FLOWERS BLOOMING

The Spring

Rishu

ISBN

Paperback 979-8-89984-521-5
Hardcase 979-8-89984-522-2

To Those Who Fuel the Journey

Every endeavour begins with a spark, but it's the people beside you who keep the flame alive.

To Mamma, Papa, Atul, and Satyarth for being the constants in a world of shifting possibilities.

You've all been the quiet force behind this creation—proof that dreams thrive when shared.

With all my gratitude,
Rishu

Contents

1

"Opening Encounter"

25 —

25th Jan, 2020,

Riwa, a B.Sc. 2nd year mathematics student was excited for this day because she was going to receive an award for winning a quiz competition. She was quite happy because, after waiting for a long time, she finally had the chance to go on stage and receive an award.

It had been many years since she last received an award on stage, so she felt a bit nervous and excited.

After that, she put on the violet-coloured outfit she had bought for the event. She styled her hair neatly and completed her look with a black watch and a pair of sneakers. Although she has a chubby face and is quite healthy, her confidence makes her look gorgeous and gives her a graceful personality. It's around 9:30 am, and the event at the college is set to start at 11:00 am. Before heading to the college, she attended her maths coaching class, which was scheduled for 10:00 am.

Since the class lasts only an hour and the college is near her coaching class, she decided to go there first.

There, she met her friend Kriti. Kriti and Riwa are good friends - not too close, but not strangers either. According to Riwa, Kriti and she share a certain emotional understanding. After their maths class, they headed to college together because Kriti was also receiving an award. Since Kriti was also going to college, she asked Riwa to join her. Riwa thanked Kriti, and they both went to college together on her Activa.

After parking Activa in the college parking lot, they headed towards the auditorium. Riwa heard a voice call out, "Hey, Kriti." Riwa turned around and saw a boy who appeared to be a good friend of Kriti. Kriti introduced him to Riwa, saying, "Riwa, he is Ved, our classmate."

Riwa recognised him and remembered Oh! He is Ved, who had secured the first position in the mathematics quiz competition. Since Riwa and Ved were in different sections – Riwa is in M2 and Ved is in M1 – they hardly knew each other before.

Since Kriti is a mutual friend of both Riwa and Ved, she introduced them to each other. After that, the three of them proceeded towards the auditorium. Due to the chilly winter winds and fog, the chief guest was late, causing the event schedule to be adjusted.

It was now set to commence at 12 noon.

As the three of them were quite hungry, they decided to go to a resto-bar where they ordered sandwiches. Riwa, being introverted, sat quietly while Kriti and Ved enjoyed a lively conversation, reflecting their strong friendship. Kriti then informed Riwa that she and Ved were school friends.

Soon, some other classmates who had come to attend the event joined them at the resto-bar. Since the event time had been shifted, they decided to stay there and have additional snacks together while enjoying some good conversation.

Kriti said to Zoha, "Hey Zoha, I heard that you won the debate competition." Zoha replied, "Yes, I did." "Who would dare to beat a girl in an argument?" they joked, and everyone began laughing.

Rohan then added to Zoha in a teasing tone, "Just get a room for yourself."

"I'm the one receiving the Student of the Year trophy at today's event," Rohan said. Ved then remarked to Rohan, "Actually, they felt a bit guilty because you helped them with the charity collection and other tasks. And they know you don't have a girlfriend also, so they decided to give you this award as compensation. Since you don't look too handsome to find one on your own, maybe this award will help you," he added teasingly. Ved and Rohan burst into laughter as they were best friends.

"Hello, you're Riwa, right?" asked Zoha.

Riwa wondered, "Am I really that well-known?" She inquired, "How do you know my name?"

Zoha responded with a smile, "I read it on the ID card you're wearing."

Zoha, Rohan, Ved, and Kriti appeared to be a close-knit group of friends. Riwa felt somewhat isolated as she couldn't join their conversation.

As it was already 12:15 PM, Rohan said, "Let's go. It's a quarter past 12, and the chief guest must be arriving soon. We should make our way to the hall."

They settled the bill at the resto-bar and moved towards the hall. As the event was about to start, the choir began singing a welcome song for the chief guest. The back-row seats were unoccupied, so they decided to take those. Afterwards, Riwa asked Kriti, "Who will take our photos when we are receiving our awards?"

Ved said, "Don't worry, I have a phone." Kriti added, "Yes, he will take all the pictures because his brother recently gifted him a smartphone with an excellent back camera." Riwa replied, "Okay." Kriti then handed her phone to Ayush, asking him to take some pictures when they were on stage. Ayush was the event coordinator for today's event and it seemed he liked Kriti, but to Kriti, he was just a friend.

After the welcome song and dance, students from each department were called one by one to receive their certificates and awards. Since there were 50 departments in the college and everyone was receiving awards for their specific categories, the five of them were waiting eagerly for their turn.

The event management team had already informed them that after the cultural department students, they would get an award. Zoha, Rohan, Kriti, Riwa, and Ved were excited. Kriti suggested, "Let's go and stand in the front." Kriti, Ved, Zoha, and Rohan agreed, and they started moving towards the stage.

Riwa tried to move to the front but found herself stuck in a crowd of senior students who had gathered. The crowd was dense, with everyone pushing against each other. Riwa was trying to find a way out when she noticed that all of her friends were standing near the stage, struggling to make space for herself, but she failed to reach them.

At that moment, Ved realised that Riwa was not with them and began searching for her to see where she was.

Riwa saw Ved making his way towards her, clearing the crowd and asking if she was alright. He instructed her to follow him so they could reach the stage. Riwa was amazed and surprised, realising he had come back for her. Both of them reached the stage, collected their awards with their friends, and took pictures. After the event, they all returned home.

In the evening, around 7:00 p.m., when Kriti shared all the pictures with Riwa, Riwa looked through them and recalled how heroically Ved had come to her and protected her. She found herself blushing, thinking how cute Ved is.

Here, Riwa actually developed feelings for Ved. She decided that if they met again, she would try to be his friend.

Since the B.Sc. exams were scheduled after the event, the college had granted a one-week preparation leave. Under the intense pressure of the exams, Riwa completely forgot about Ved and focused solely on her studies.

2
"The Lockdown Phase"

24ᵗʰ March 2020,

B.Sc. exams are over now, and everyone is enjoying their post-exam break and feeling happy. Suddenly, a new announcement reveals that a lockdown will be imposed across India starting from tomorrow. Riwa was watching this news with her family. Her family consists of three members: her mother, her father, and a younger brother.

Everyone at Riwa's house was discussing the lockdown. A few days ago, Riwa's grandmother came to visit her, and due to the lockdown, she is now staying with Riwa. Although Riwa's grandmother normally lives in Allahabad with her aunt, but now she will remain at Riwa's house because of the lockdown. She has lots of love for her grandchildren.

Everything appears nice and simple in Riwa's family, but Riwa's life is not as straightforward as it seems. There are many hidden secrets beneath the surface. While Riwa's family might appear financially stable, they are dealing with numerous mental and emotional challenges.

Riwa's house is a two-story building. On the ground floor, her uncle and aunt live, while Riwa's family resides on the first floor. Everything seems so beautiful and sweet from the outside, but we don't know what it's really like inside. Even though it appears that they live together as a joint family, enjoying festivals and maintaining open relationships, issues within relationships often lead to problems.

Riwa's family is also facing similar struggles. Riwa's uncle and aunt have two daughters: the elder one is a government teacher and the younger one is a freelancer. Both earn well, and the couple is financially stable. However, when greed overshadows relationships, they can deteriorate. This situation also affects Riwa's family, where greed overshadows their family values.

Riwa's aunt wants to split the family and sell the house so that each family can receive their share, although both parties are good enough. But in Riwa's family, Riwa is a college student and her brother is in school. Because of these reasons, her father doesn't want to sell the house at the crucial stage of their life. On the contrary, Riwa's aunt's daughters are financially independent and in their mid-twenties. Riwa's father is deeply unhappy and upset by the idea of selling the house as it holds 20 years of memories, from his marriage to raising his children. He is reluctant to part with it but is pressured by his own family's demands.

If Riwa's family refuses to sell the house, her aunt threatens to file a police complaint against them. Her aunt is also threatening that if they do not agree to her terms, she will involve their children in the police case.

Riwa's family is not afraid of this; her aunt has some connections with underground goons. Fearing potential trouble, Riwa's father agreed to the demands because he wanted to avoid getting entangled in any dangerous situations.

Riwa's father finally agrees to sell the house despite his reluctance. He treasures the house deeply, recognising it as his 'third child' filled with precious memories. He prioritised his two children over it. This decision has deeply upset him, but he felt he had no other choice. No matter how much he values the house, family comes first, and he cannot change his circumstances.

Just a day before the paperwork of the house, Riwa realised at night that after tomorrow, this house would no longer be theirs. Someone else would live here and someone else would laugh within these walls. This realisation brought a flood of memories, flashing back to how they had witnessed everything here, how they had faced every situation. She remembered the lockdown days when there was nothing to do, and everyone would gather in the living room to play Ludo. All these memories came rushing back to her.

Riwa wanted to cry, but she couldn't. If she started crying, all her family members would be heartbroken and would share her sorrow. So, she controlled her emotions and projected an image of emotional strength. She knew that as the eldest daughter, she had to be brave and resilient to support and sustain her family through this challenging time.

Finally, the day had arrived when they went to the court to sign the papers and finalise the sale of their house. The property was transferred to the new owner, and each family received their share. They all moved to a new residence. Riwa and her family found a house to rent in a different area because the lockdown was still in effect, and restrictions prevented movement between cities. As a result, Riwa's grandmother decided to stay with them instead of moving back to her aunt's house.

None of the family members was happy with the situation, but they realised that they couldn't change their fate. Gradually, everything began to settle down after a week.

Since Riwa had already moved into the rented house, they shifted their belongings and began arranging the new place according to their needs.

While none was truly content, there was. They understood that facing the challenges ahead was inevitable, and there was no benefit in dwelling on the past. Now, Riwa's family was focusing on their next step, knowing they couldn't stay in a rented house forever.

They were determined to find and purchase their own home, and everyone was thinking about how to make that happen.

3

"The Hustle"

It had been almost a month of living in the rented house, but not a whole month had passed without challenges. Setting things up was not easy, as no one was accustomed to the new living situation. Adjusting to the water amenities posed some difficulties, but everyone was finding ways to adapt. Now, each person was busy managing their own life and schedules, and their things were gradually returning to normal. Life was becoming easier with the reopening of businesses and institutions, and things were starting to get back on track.

During this time, the B.Sc. 2nd year's result was released, and she had passed with good marks. Afterwards, she decided to contact Kriti to enquire about the college class schedule and the formalities for the third year of B.Sc. That evening, they asked about each other's well-being and how everything was going.

They then started discussing college matters, such as the timing of practicals. While the situation with COVID-19 had improved, many precautions were still necessary, and as a result, classes could continue to be held online.

They had been chatting about the usual things - online schedules, third-year admissions, and the everyday chaos of life - when suddenly Kriti mentioned Ved's name.

Riwa's heart skipped a beat.

For a moment, everything about her faded. The sound of Kriti's voice became distant, replaced by the echo of a name she hadn't thought about in a long time.

Ved.

How had she let him slip from her mind?

A wave of guilt crept in, tightening around the chest.

"He was hospitalised recently," Kriti continued, her voice carrying an unspoken concern. "He was not keeping well."

The words landed like a heavy weight on Riwa's shoulder. Hospitalised? Her fingers clenched around the phone in the struggle to process it.

"How... How is he now?" she asked, her voice barely above a whisper.

"He's better," Kriti reassured her. "Discharged yesterday. I spoke to him last night - he said he's doing fine, just recovering."

A breath Riwa hadn't realised she was holding escaped her lips.

Relief, yes - but it was laced with regret. She had been so caught up in her own life that she hadn't even known what Ved was going through.

Wasn't this the same person who once understood her without words? How had she let their connection fade into nothingness?

Their conversation eventually shifted to lighter topics: shared laughter, old memories, but Riwa felt distant, her mind tangled in emotions she didn't quite know how to name.

After the call ended, she sat in silence, her phone resting loosely in her hand. An unsettling thought took root. She needed to check on Ved herself, to hear his voice, to know - really know - that he was okay.

But then, hesitation crept in. She didn't have his number.

Her fingers hovered over the screen, debating whether to ask Kriti for it. It was such a simple thing - just one message - but why did it feel so heavy? Would Ved even want to hear from her? Had too much time passed, too many silences settled between them?

She sighed, leaning back against the wall. The night stretched around her, quiet and still.

Her thumb moved towards Kriti's contact, but just before she could type, she stopped. Instead, she placed the phone on the table and stared at the screen, as if waiting for an answer that only time would give.

Some distances weren't meant to be closed in a single moment.

Riwa hesitated, running different scenarios through her mind. What would she say when she called Ved? She decided to keep it simple - just a quick check on his well-being. But even as she settled on that, doubt crept in. What if he asked how she found out?

"She thought she could tell him that Kriti had mentioned him on the call."

She shook off the thought. Checking in on someone was normal.

They knew each other, after all. Still, another worry surfaced - what if Ved didn't even remember her? They had only met once, and she had noticed his struggle with remembering names. If that was the case, would he ask, "Who is Riwa? Sorry, I forgot?"

Her fingers hovered over the call button. Why was something so simple suddenly so difficult? She had always been shy, always second-guessing herself. Conversations never came easily - words tangled in her mind before they could make it out. The fear of saying the wrong thing, of sounding awkward, held her back more often than she liked to admit.

She sighed, setting her phone down. Overthinking wouldn't change anything. In the end, it didn't really matter – after all, they were going to meet the day after tomorrow for admission. Maybe that was enough.

The next morning, Riwa walked into the bustling college campus, a mix of excitement and restlessness swirling inside her. She had completed the admission formalities for her B.Sc. third year, but her mind was preoccupied with a different thought - would Ved be there today?

The college had assigned students different sections based on their subjects, and with the admission deadline extended, there was no guarantee that she would not run into him. She glanced around, scanning the crowd, hoping for a glimpse of his familiar presence. But with every passing moment, anticipation gave way to quiet disappointment. Maybe he had chosen a different day. Maybe she wouldn't see him at all.

Still, hope flickered. If not today, then some other day, she reassured herself before focusing back on the admission process. Once everything was completed, she made her way home, her thoughts lingering on the unanswered question—when would they meet again?

A few days later, the new academic year began, but not in the way anyone had imagined.

Instead of stepping into lecture halls, students found themselves staring at computer screens. Online classes had taken over, and while the shift felt surreal, it was also unsettling for many, especially the professors; this sudden change was unfamiliar territory.

Students whispered among themselves, wondering how their teachers would handle the new format. Technology was supposed to bridge the gap, but could it replace the warmth of a classroom?

Could it truly capture the essence of learning?

Riwa, like many others, had these doubts. Would they be able to adjust? Would she? As the first virtual lecture began, she took a deep breath, realising that this was not just a new academic year; it was an entirely new way of learning, one that would test them all in unexpected ways.

Online classes often felt like a test of patience.

Network glitches, muffled voices, and the occasional screech of an unmuted microphone turned learning into a struggle. Some sessions dragged on, but chemistry was an exception. The young professor brought a spark to his lesson, making even the periodic table seem alive.

Mathematics, however, was a different story. The professors, though experienced, clung to their old ways, making the subject feel like a heavy textbook with no illustrations. Students often exchanged glances, silently questioning if tradition always equalled wisdom. Yet they reassured themselves, "Old is gold," convincing their restless minds that experience still held value.

One professor, in particular, stood out — not for his teaching style, but for the nickname students had given him, "Doramon." His bald head and animated expressions turned him into a campus legend. The moment he logged in, a playful murmur would spread — "Doramon is here, pay attention!" The humour, though lighthearted, made the online months a little more bearable.

Meanwhile, practical classes brought their own challenges. Scheduled in batches of 20, the students navigated a whirlwind of exposures on different days. The structure was chaotic, but at least it brought a break from the screen fatigue of virtual lectures.

One evening, when Riwa was studying, suddenly an idea sparked in her mind: 'What if I teach?'

The thought lingered, hesitant at first, then firm. She knew she couldn't change her family's struggles overnight, but she could lighten the load.

With quiet determination, she made her decision. The very next day, she arranged her books neatly, took a deep breath and tidied her room.

As Riwa picked up her pen to write, she realised that life's most valuable lessons often came in quiet moments of determination. Already tutoring her brother, she began teaching neighbourhood children to help her parents and earn some pocket money.

With B.Sc. classes in the morning and tuitions in the evening, her days blurred into nights – a relentless cycle of study and teaching, leaving her little time to breathe.

4

"It's Celebration Time"

The entire year passed, yet Riwa never got a chance to meet Ved. Their schedules were completely different, and the only time she was allowed on campus was during her practical sessions. Strict COVID-19 regulations made things even more challenging. The college enforced these rules rigidly, allowing students on campus only with valid authorisation. Those scheduled for practicals on a given day could attend, while anyone found without permission faced strict penalties.

As a result, Riwa and Ved remained apart the entire year. Time flew by, and before she knew it, the year was drawing to a close. Just two months before exams, an unexpected decision by the third-year students set events into motion that no one had anticipated.

The college decided to hold a farewell party as COVID-19 was nearing its end, and things were beginning to settle down. After one and a half years without any celebrations, the students were eager to enjoy the occasion. The college also agreed to let them organise the event.

While everyone was excited, Riwa, who had been unwell a week before the party, contributed financially but did not take part in any cultural activities. She had simply planned to attend and witness the farewell celebrations. Finally, the much-awaited day arrived.

Riwa was feeling better and getting ready for the farewell party. As the bright noon sun streamed through her window, she carefully put on her elegant dress, feeling a quiet anticipation. Her mother gave her a subtle makeup look that enhanced her natural beauty. A touch of eyeliner defined her expressive eyes, while her graceful posture and delicate collarbones subtly added to her charm.

As she glanced in the mirror, a soft smile appeared on her face. Today, she wasn't just an observer—she was stepping into the celebration, ready to embrace the afternoon ahead.

As she prepared for the event, she hoped to finally meet Ved since everyone would be there. She reflected on how the entire year had passed without a chance to talk to him. Today might be their last opportunity. With exams scheduled for different sections, another chance seemed unlikely.

Although she wished for a deeper bond with Ved, she knew this would likely be their final conversation. After the farewell party, everyone would be engrossed in their careers, and life would move on. Accepting this reality, she chose to focus on making good memories and hoped for a pleasant, unforgettable day. She understood that not everyone ends up with their crush, so she embraced the moment and moved forward.

When Riwa arrived at the college, she spotted Prashant at the gate. He greeted her with a warm smile and said, "You look beautiful today, Riwa. I can't take my eyes off you."

Riwa chuckled, shaking her head. "Oh, stop it, Prashant. Let's go—everyone's waiting, and we're already late."

Prashant added with a teasing smile, "You know, we boys are like the college's unpaid helpers—always setting up for events and running around. Meanwhile, the girls just show up looking fresh and stylish while we're left sweating away. It seems a bit unfair, doesn't it?"

Riwa smiled and replied, "Okay, okay, just go and bring the stuff! Come back soon so we can have a great time today. Don't let this spoil your mood. And thanks for being the event's unpaid peon," she joked.

They both laughed, and before leaving, Prashant said to Riwa, "Go on ahead to the auditorium. I'll be back quickly—with a bouquet of lovely roses just for you!"

Riwa laughed and shook her head. "You won't change, will you? You flirt with every girl, but trust me; it won't work on me."

They laughed again and then went their separate ways.

5
"Embracing New Beginnings"

As Riwa stepped into the bustling auditorium, the air was thick with excitement and the hum of conversations. Her eyes scanned the crowd until they settled on Swati, her good friend, waving enthusiastically from across the room. A smile broke across her face as she made her way through the sea of students.

They shared a quick hug before diving into a lively conversation about the much-anticipated event. But something about Swati's smile seemed off—strained, her eyes darting nervously. Finally, she sighed and spoke, her shoulders slumping. "I have to leave early. Mom needs me back home, and I can't stay for the entire programme."

The cheerful expression faltered. "Oh... That's disappointing. But... I get it." She tried to mask her letdown with an encouraging smile, but her tone betrayed her sadness. A knowing glance passed between them, a silent acknowledgement of the inevitable.

Determined to enjoy the time they had, they settled into their seats. The auditorium dazzled with decorations—colourful balloons swaying from the ceiling, shimmering lights tracing delicate patterns along the walls, and a large banner with "Farewell and New Beginnings" hanging proudly over the stage.

The programme began with a melodious welcome song, the singer's voice rich and soothing. A graceful classical dance followed, every movement precise and elegant, drawing applause from the audience. Clapping along, she felt her earlier disappointment begin to ease.

As the spotlight shifted, her gaze followed. The anchors—Ved and Zoha—stood confidently on stage, exchanging witty remarks with flawless timing that left the audience laughing. Their effortless chemistry spoke of countless rehearsals, and she couldn't help but admire their coordination.

A pang of longing twisted in her heart. That should have been her up there, sharing the stage with Ved, guiding the audience through the evening's excitement. But the fever that had kept her bedridden through rehearsals had snatched the opportunity away.

She tried to ignore the thought, but it clawed at her mind, stubbornly refusing to be ignored. Instead, she focused on the lively performances, the energy of the crowd slowly pulling her back into the moment.

The dramatic sketch that followed was a hilarious parody of classroom life, complete with exaggerated teacher impersonations and cheeky student antics. Laughter erupted throughout the hall, even from the teachers who shook their heads with amused resignation.

Yet, her gaze kept drifting back to the stage. Ved's laughter was unrestrained, his eyes crinkling with genuine amusement. The sight stirred something within her—a blend of admiration and a deeper longing she could never quite banish. She forced herself to look away, scolding her foolishness.

After the drama, the hall was filled with the soulful strumming of a guitar, its melody weaving seamlessly with the singer's voice to create a serene, almost magical atmosphere. For a moment, Riwa closed her eyes, letting the music wash over her, easing the ache of her disappointment.

But tranquillity soon gave way to a burst of energy as dance performances took over the stage. The dancers' enthusiasm was infectious, their coordinated moves earning cheers and applause from the crowd. Riwa found herself clapping along, her spirits gradually lifting.

Then came the mimicry segment. Students imitated their teachers' mannerisms with exaggerated accuracy, their impressions sparking howls of laughter from everyone present. Even the teachers themselves joined in the applause, their smiles broad and forgiving.

Laughter spilled from her lips freely, mingling with the cheerful noise around her. For a while, the regret of missed opportunities seemed like a distant shadow.

As the performances wrapped up, refreshments were served, and conversations bubbled up from all directions, the mingling of voices creating a comforting background hum. Light-hearted chatter and shared jokes made her forget, if only briefly, the nagging thoughts that had haunted her all afternoon.

But the most emotional part of the evening was yet to come. The final-year B.Sc. Mathematics students gathered on stage, their voices trembling with emotion as they shared memories of their college years. Nostalgia clung to every word; their speeches were a blend of gratitude, sadness, and hope.

"We may be leaving these halls," one of them said, the voice thick and filled with emotion. "But the bonds we've made will stay with us forever. No matter where life takes us, these memories will remain."

Applause echoed through the hall, but the heaviness of goodbyes pressed down on everyone. Yet, there was warmth in that heaviness, a reminder that partings were only a chapter in a much larger story.

As the audience began to disperse and refreshments dwindled, Riwa remained seated, her gaze lingering on the stage. Disappointment still clung to her, but it no longer felt like a crushing weight.

The event had finally ended, with echoes of laughter and applause still hanging in the air. The hall was gradually emptying as students began to drift out in groups, their chatter blending into a low, cheerful hum. On stage, the organisers were busy gathering props, folding banners, and clearing away the remnants of the evening's celebration.

Zoha, Ved, Rishit, Kriti, Prashant, Priyam, Rohan, Sana, and Bela were all occupied with packing up. Their voices intermingled with the rustle of paper and the clinking of chairs being rearranged. Riwa watched them from a distance, her eyes drawn almost instinctively to Ved, who seemed to be giving instructions while chuckling over something Zoha had said.

Riwa wanted to speak to him and share even a brief moment of conversation before everything dispersed into memory. But every time she took a step forward, her courage wavered. After all, everyone was too busy wrapping up the event to pay attention to anything else.

Riwa turned to Kriti, who was struggling to untangle a set of decorative lights. "Kriti, let's leave together," Riwa suggested, her voice a little too eager. "It's our last day in college before the exams start, and who knows when we'll meet again. Let's all go together."

Kriti glanced at her, her face lighting up with relief. "Yes, of course! I'll leave with you. Just give me a few more minutes to sort out this mess. Once everything's packed up, we'll head out together."

Riwa smiled and pitched in to help. They carefully folded the decorations, gathered scattered papers, and stacked chairs. It wasn't long before the task became almost enjoyable, their shared efforts punctuated by casual conversation.

Everything seemed to be winding down when Rohan's voice rang out in sudden panic. "Oh no! I forgot to give these roses to the teachers!" He held up a bundle of red roses, their petals slightly wilted from being neglected during the noontime bustle. "We brought these to make the teachers feel special during the welcome ceremony, and I completely forgot!"

Ved's laughter came swift and light. "Rohan, how could you forget? You made such a big deal about bringing these roses. How can you be so absent-minded?" His eyes sparkled with amusement as he folded his arms over his chest.

Rohan rubbed the back of his neck sheepishly. "I know, I know. My bad. Guess I was too caught up with everything else."

Zoha joined in with a smirk. "Well, it's not like you don't have a chance to fix it. Why don't you go and give them to the teachers now?"

"That's the plan," Rohan said, his shoulders relaxing. "But I'll need some help if I'm going to catch everyone before they leave." His gaze swept over the group, landing on Riwa and Kriti, who were still clearing up some remaining decorations. "Would you two mind helping me?"

"Sure," Riwa replied, grateful for the distraction. Anything to keep her from glancing at Ved every other minute. "Let's get this done."

The trio moved quickly through the scattered crowd, handing out roses to the teachers who were still around. The expressions of delight and appreciation they received made Rohan's oversight seem almost like a blessing. Even Riwa felt her spirits lift as teachers offered kind words of encouragement for their future.

When the last rose was handed over, Riwa took a moment to breathe. The hall was almost empty now, the event reduced to nothing but traces of decorations and fading voices. As she turned back toward the stage area, her eyes met Ved's again. He was still engaged in conversation with Zoha and Rishit, his expression animated.

Before she could talk herself out of it, she approached the group, her steps feeling heavier than they should. "Hey, Ved," she called softly, her voice barely rising above the murmur of conversations.

He turned, surprise flickering across his face before it softened into a warm smile. "Hey, Riwa! Have you guys finished handing out the roses?"

"Yeah, all sorted," she replied, forcing herself to meet his gaze. "I just... I just wanted to say that you and Zoha did a great job hosting the event. It was amazing to watch."

"Thanks," Ved replied, his eyes brightening with genuine gratitude. "I was nervous about it. But Zoha made everything so much easier."

"She's good at that," Riwa admitted, glancing briefly at Zoha, who was now chatting with Rishit. "But I'm sure you would've done great even on your own."

Ved chuckled, rubbing his neck in a way that seemed almost shy. "I appreciate the vote of confidence. And by the way, I heard you were supposed to be my co-anchor before... you know, you got sick."

The mention of her missed opportunity made her heart sink a little, but she pushed the feeling aside. "Yeah. But I guess things worked out just fine without me."

"Maybe," Ved said, his gaze holding hers. "But I was looking forward to hosting with you. You have this way of making everything seem perfect, even when it's not."

Her cheeks flushed at his words, the warmth spreading through her chest like sunlight breaking through clouds. "Well, maybe there'll be another chance someday," she murmured, her voice wavering between hope and uncertainty.

"Maybe," Ved replied with a smile that seemed to promise something more. "I guess we'll just have to see."

The world felt a little lighter at that moment, as if the weight of disappointment had finally begun to lift.

Just as Riwa gathered her courage to continue the conversation with Ved, a voice called out from across the courtyard.

"Ved! Come here for a minute," one of the event coordinators shouted, waving a file in his hand.

Ved glanced at Riwa, an apologetic smile tugging at his lips. "Sorry, duty calls. I'll be right back."

Before Riwa could respond, he jogged off towards the coordinator, his footsteps echoing against the cobblestone path. She watched him go, her nerves a tangled mess. It felt like she had been so close to something — a moment of clarity, perhaps. But now, the air between them had shifted, the hesitation clawing its way back in.

With nothing else to do, she took out her phone and scrolled through the photos she had taken during the event. Pictures of smiling faces, dance performances frozen in mid-motion, and, of course, a few candid shots of Ved on stage, his face lit with enthusiasm.

"Enjoying the memories?" Kriti's voice cut through her thoughts, her tone light and teasing.

Riwa grinned sheepishly. "Just going through the pictures. It all went by so fast."

"It really did," Kriti sighed, glancing over her shoulder at the dispersing crowd. "It feels strange, doesn't it? Knowing this was probably our last big event before exams and then... who knows what?"

The words sank into Riwa's mind, heavy and unshakeable. Everyone was moving on, chasing dreams and ambitions that would soon carry them far beyond the college gates. The thought of losing touch with the people she cared about, especially Ved, was a hollow ache she couldn't ignore.

"Yeah, it does feel strange," Riwa admitted. "But I guess that's just part of moving forward."

Moments later, Kriti asked Riwa, "Let's leave. It's getting late, and you know how deserted my area gets after dark. We should go."

Riwa glanced over at Ved one last time. He was still engrossed in conversation, his laughter ringing like music in her ears. Swallowing her disappointment, she nodded, "Yeah, let's go."

Their walk home was quiet, the cool evening air thick with words left unsaid. Kriti finally broke the silence. "You should have tried talking to him. Even if it's just to say goodbye."

"I know," Riwa admitted. "But every time I try, my words just... disappear. It's like I've built this barrier around myself, and no matter how hard I try, I can't break through."

Kriti squeezed her shoulder. "Maybe you're just scared of what happens after you speak. But you can't keep letting fear hold you back."

Riwa offered a weak smile. "Maybe. But it's not like I'll get another chance now."

The night crept on. Standing alone on her terrace, she let the cool breeze brush against her skin. The stars above seemed indifferent to her silent struggle. She couldn't help but feel frustrated with herself. Why couldn't she be like Kriti? Confident, unafraid, and unapologetically herself.

But a small voice inside her refused to be silenced. Maybe this moment of failure was necessary. Maybe she needed to confront her own weaknesses before she could grow.

The next morning, as Riwa sat at the breakfast table, her mother asked, "So, what are your plans after graduation?"

Riwa had been dreading this question, but the answer came surprisingly easily. "I want to teach. I've always enjoyed my tutoring sessions. Watching students grasp something they once struggled with... It feels fulfilling."

Her mother's expression softened, a proud smile curving her lips. "That sounds like a wonderful plan. You've always had the patience and kindness for it."

"Maybe... maybe if I can help others find their confidence, I'll find mine along the way," Riwa replied, her voice steady and resolute.

For the first time, her future didn't feel like an empty canvas. She had a purpose. And perhaps, somewhere down the line, she would gather the strength to face the emotions she had locked away.

Because some journeys don't start with someone else; they start from within.

6

"The Unexpected Journey"

Riwa's final year result was finally announced, marking the completion of her graduation journey. She had excelled once again, her remarkable performance filling her family with pride. But for Riwa, this was just the beginning. With graduation now behind her, she was ready to focus entirely on her future studies.

Her immediate goal was to clear the All-India Teacher Eligibility Entrance Exam (AIEEEE), a stepping stone that she believed would lead her to a reputed government college.

Riwa had always dreamed of securing admission to Dronacharya College, a distinguished institution renowned for its exceptional teaching programme and extensive support through government facilities. The college's faculty, known for their unmatched expertise and guidance, made it the ideal place to pursue her ambitions.

Driven by her aspirations, Riwa devoted herself wholeheartedly to her preparation, her determination unwavering as she worked tirelessly to make her dreams a reality.

The entrance exam had consumed Riwa's days and nights. It was the shared ambition of countless aspiring educators, but for Riwa, the goal of securing admission to Dronacharya College—one of the most esteemed institutions in India for teacher training—was not just a dream. It was her destiny.

The day had finally arrived. Riwa spent the previous night double-checking her notes, her eyes heavy yet relentless. That morning, her hands moved with a precision born of routine, gathering every essential item she would need. Yet, her fingers trembled like leaves caught in a gentle breeze, betraying the nerves churning within her.

Before she left, her mother called her into the kitchen, offering her a spoonful of yoghurt and sugar. The gesture was more than a simple tradition; it was her mother's way of pouring all her love, blessings, and hopes into a single act. As Riwa swallowed the cool, sweet mixture, she felt a surge of warmth and strength flood her veins—a quiet assurance that she wasn't alone in her journey.

Her father drove her to the exam centre, his protective gaze lingering even as they arrived. "I'll wait here, beta. Just call me when you're done."

Riwa's lips curved into a determined smile. "No, Papa," she replied, her voice steady and certain. "I need to do this on my own."

It was more than a refusal; it was a declaration of her readiness to face the world without fear. Her father nodded, a hint of pride gleaming in his eyes, as Riwa walked towards the centre, her heart pounding but her resolve stronger than ever.

The college campus buzzed with nervous energy. Students poured in from every direction, their anxious murmurs blending into a chaotic hum. Riwa scanned the display board, her eyes darting over the crowded lists until she found her assigned classroom.

She followed the signs to the locker room and handed over her belongings, receiving a small coupon in return. The paper felt fragile between her fingers, yet she clung to it as if it were her only anchor.

The security checks were relentless. Guards scanned admission cards, scrutinised identification, and checked for any unauthorised materials. The process was slow, draining, and felt more like a mental test than a physical one. But Riwa moved through it all with calm precision, her focus narrowing with each step.

Finally, she passed the last checkpoint and made her way towards the assigned classroom. The air felt cool and sterile, the chill of the air conditioning prickling her skin. As she walked, the muffled rustle of papers and faint echoes of whispers grew louder.

Approaching the invigilator's desk, she presented her admit card. The stern-looking woman gave it a swift glance before nodding and pointing her towards a seat. The metal chair was cold and uncomfortable, but Riwa settled into it, her fingers trembling slightly as she adjusted her pen on the desk.

For a moment, the world seemed to blur. Thoughts rushed through her mind, snippets of formulas and theories flashing like lightning. Did I study enough? What if I forgot something important? But beneath the panic, a stronger voice pushed through. You've worked hard for this, Riwa. Just breathe.

The silence in the room was thick, punctuated only by the occasional shuffling of feet and rustling of papers. She took a deep breath, feeling the cold air fill her lungs, grounding her in the present moment.

Finally, the exam began.

The exam was a beast, split into two merciless parts: Section A tested general knowledge, language, and reasoning, while Section B drilled deep into subject-specific content. For Riwa, it meant wrestling with complex maths and science problems. Her pen danced over the paper, driven by restless nights of preparation and the relentless dream of making it to Dronacharya College.

When she finally surrendered her answer sheet, a mix of relief and dread tangled within her. She had done her best, but was it enough? The weight of her aspirations bore down heavily on her chest.

The results were scheduled to be announced on 29th October — a date branded into her memory like a blazing mark. The days crawled by, her mind replaying every tricky question, every moment of hesitation as if she could rewrite her answers with sheer will.

The morning of October 29th arrived, thick with tension. Riwa's fingers trembled as she refreshed the results page over and over, her phone screen glowing like a cruel tease. Hours melted away, her nerves fraying with each failed attempt to load the results. News of a server crash spread quickly, only deepening her frustration.

"Just have faith, Riwa. You've done your best. Whatever happens, we're there for you," her mother said.

The entire day slipped away in restless agony. Her phone lay abandoned on her bed, surrounded by a sea of crumpled notes and textbooks. Her heart felt hollow, and her mind was trapped in a spiral of doubt.

Night crept in, the silence almost suffocating. Then, out of nowhere, her phone vibrated. A single notification — the result was finally out.

With shaky hands and a racing heartbeat, Riwa opened the website, the glow of the screen illuminating her anxious eyes. Everything she had worked for came down to this single moment.

Riwa anxiously opened her laptop and typed in her admit card number. Her heartbeat quickened as she awaited the result. The screen loaded, revealing her rank—50k out of 6 lakh candidates. The disappointment stung, but the rank was enough for the initial round of counselling. Still, her dream of getting into Dronacharya College seemed distant.

Her parents encouraged her to be patient and strategic. "I'll take my time to research the best options during the first round of counselling," Riwa assured them, her voice steady but her mind restless. They respected her decision, letting her navigate her path.

Days slipped by as Riwa meticulously prepared her list of preferred colleges, triple-checking every detail. But when the counselling results were announced, her eyes widened in disbelief. She had mistakenly ranked Shree College higher than Gurukul College, her true second choice. The realisation crashed over her like icy water.

Frustration and panic tangled within her. How could she have made such a careless mistake? She stared at the screen, her chest tightening with regret. She struggled to find the words to tell her parents, her fingers trembling over the keyboard.

Disheartened, Riwa broke the news to her parents that evening. Their disappointment was palpable as they questioned her carelessness. Apologising, she sought their guidance, torn between reapplying or accepting the reality of her mistake. Reluctantly, Riwa decided to proceed with admission to Shree College, worried that waiting for the next round of counselling might leave her without a seat at all.

The following day, she completed the admission formalities at Shree College, resigning herself to her circumstances. As she tried to come to terms with her new reality, Riwa's parents voiced concerns about her daily commute to the college, which was situated on the outskirts of the city. They feared for her safety and vulnerability, knowing she had always been somewhat naive.

Riwa assured them that facing these challenges was inevitable. Sooner or later, she would have to navigate the world on her own. Though anxious, her parents acknowledged her determination and reluctantly supported her decision.

Days passed, and although she was still disheartened by the twist of fate, Riwa focused on moving forward. Her parents noted her calm acceptance with mixed feelings—worried about her tendency to suppress her disappointments yet proud of her resilience.

One evening, Riwa called Swati, her old friend who was now pursuing business studies. Their conversation was warm and comforting, with Riwa finding solace in Swati's encouragement. They both agreed to meet someday and delve into conversations that extended beyond their hurried phone calls.

Soon after, Riwa received a message welcoming her to Shree College of Teacher Education. The realisation hit her—this was her new beginning. While life had veered from her initial plan, it offered her an opportunity to grow, explore, and perhaps even discover a new version of herself.

Riwa smiled at the thought. Her heart brimmed with hope and quiet determination. The adventure had just begun.

7

"Chatter Clash"

Riwa stood at the bus stop, heart racing, her father's words echoing in her mind. Around her, students buzzed with nervous excitement. The bus arrived—her first step into the unknown.

Inside, she met Swarna and Sanvi. Strangers at first, yet something clicked. Words flowed, fears eased, and by the time they reached Shree College, they weren't just passengers—they were companions on a shared journey.

The grand gates loomed. The campus felt vast, alive with possibility. In the playground, the inaugural assembly began. "Future Forward: We Are the Future of India," the banner read.

As Riwa stood among countless students, she felt it – a quiet certainty. This was where she was meant to be.

The event was a spectacle of passionate performances and stirring melodies, setting an inspiring tone for the day. Following the assembly, students gathered in class, where the teacher meticulously outlined the syllabus, detailing schedules, practical sessions, creative assignments, and extracurricular activities. The structure was well-organised, though the absence of a few students slightly diminished the collective enthusiasm.

After a two-hour lecture, a break at one o'clock offered relief. Despite the open cafeteria, students unpacked their homemade lunches, a lingering habit from the pandemic. The air filled with laughter and familiar aromas, evoking school-day nostalgia. In that shared moment, the new academic journey felt both fresh and comfortingly familiar.

After lunch, an announcement was sent to students scrambling—Aadhaar copies were due by the end of the day. Some rushed to print, others called home, and time slipped away unnoticed.

As the day ended, Sanvi and Agami left first, followed by Swarna and Riwa. The day had been neither remarkable nor dull, just a quiet beginning. That evening, friend requests and messages flooded their phones, forging a digital bond that soon extended to their daily commute.

Sanvi had a passion for technology but attended college only under parental pressure. Agami, consumed by government job exam prep, became increasingly distant; only Swarna and Riwa remained. Swarna guides Riwa like an elder sister, filling the gaps in her knowledge.

One morning, at the bus stop, they spotted a teacher beside his stalled car. After a brief hesitation, Riwa greeted him warmly. He looked up, surprised, then smiled in return. As the bus arrived, they boarded together—slipping into the rhythm of college life, where every day felt familiar yet quietly uncertain.

They took the same bus to college. Upon arrival, Swarna advised Riwa against greeting teachers on public transport, explaining that some might not appreciate it. Riwa disagreed, leading to a brief argument. However, after some reflection, she acknowledged Swarna's perspective while choosing to stay true to her own beliefs.

Over time, they befriended classmates like Anvi, Urvi, Tia, and Anne, all of whom were warm and friendly. They soon joined the same WhatsApp group, strengthening their bond beyond the classroom.

Tia was one of the most admired girls in college. Known for her flawless makeup and striking presence, she carried herself with effortless charm. A delicate mole on her left cheek added to her allure, and her bold lip colours became a signature, highlighting her magnetic appeal. Regardless of complexion, her beauty was undeniable, captivating both boys and girls alike.

Anne, on the other hand, was the group's beauty expert. Skilled in makeup artistry, she frequently gave tutorials to her friends, transforming even the simplest looks into something extraordinary. With a keen eye for detail and a passion for creativity, she became everyone's go-to for styling tips, adding a spark of glamour to their daily lives.

As the days passed, their circle grew stronger, bound not just by shared classes but by the quiet understanding that college was more than academics – it was about friendships, choices, and the confidence to be oneself.

Boys often saw Tia as their dream girl, drawn to her effortless charm and striking beauty. She enjoyed the attention and knew exactly how to leverage it. Tia had a way of accepting favours without hesitation, always aware of how to use her allure to her advantage.

Riwa, however, remained wary. Though she maintained a friendly relationship with Tia, an unshakeable unease lingered beneath the surface. At first, she wondered if it was jealousy—Tia's looks, her effortless popularity—but deep down, she knew that wasn't it. Something about Tia felt... off. A fleeting expression, a carefully measured smile—small details Riwa couldn't ignore. Yet every time she tried to understand, the feeling slipped through her grasp, like a shadow just out of reach.

Eventually, Riwa chose not to dwell on it. College was temporary, and once this brief chapter ended, their paths would likely never cross again. Wasting time trying to decipher Tia's nature seemed pointless. Still, as she walked away, she couldn't shake the lingering thought—sometimes, the most captivating things were also the hardest to truly see.

One afternoon, the group gathered in the college cafeteria, laughter and chatter filling the air as they enjoyed their lunch. The mood was light—until Tia suddenly broke the ice, her gaze settling on Riwa.

"Hey, Riwa, don't you think you should try some makeup? You'd look so much better—more attractive," she said with a playful smirk.

Riwa looked up, unfazed. "No need. I don't rely on artificial looks," she replied calmly, taking a sip of her juice.

Tia arched a brow, her smile tightening. "Oh, come on, are you jealous of my makeup look? Don't you have a boyfriend too?" Her tone carried a hint of challenge, as if daring Riwa to admit something.

Riwa met her gaze, steady and unwavering. "I don't have time for such things right now. You deserve what you have, and I deserve better, which is why I'm waiting for the right person."

A tense silence fell over the table. The playful banter had shifted, taking on an edge that wasn't there before. The others exchanged glances, sensing the conversation was heading somewhere uncomfortable.

Before the moment could escalate, Urvi, ever the peacemaker, leaned in with a bright, deliberate tone. "Riwa, could you come with me? I need your help in the library."

Riwa turned to her, slightly amused. "Urvi, do you really need my help right now? We were just getting into an interesting conversation, weren't we, Tia?"

Urvi's smile didn't waver. "Yes, I do. I have to organise the books, and I could really use an extra pair of hands. Come on, let's get it done quickly."

Riwa exhaled, glancing once more at Tia, who still held that unreadable expression. Then, with a small shrug, she stood up. "Alright, Urvi. Let's go."

As they walked away, Urvi cast a knowing glance at Riwa. "You handled that well," she whispered.

Riwa smirked. "Oh, trust me. That was just the beginning."

Riwa and Urvi stepped into the quiet library, the scent of aged paper and wooden shelves calming the air between them. Sunlight slanted through the windows, casting soft patterns on the floor.

"Alright, which books do we need to arrange?" Riwa asked, rolling up her sleeves. "Let's finish quickly so we're not late for class,"

Urvi pointed to a stack on the table. "These. Let's put them in their places carefully."

As they worked, the silence between them wasn't uncomfortable, but Riwa could tell Urvi had something on her mind. She wasn't the type to interfere unnecessarily, which meant she had deliberately pulled Riwa away from that conversation with Tia.

"You really needed my help, or was that just an escape plan?" Riwa asked, placing a book on the shelf.

Urvi smirked, not looking up. "Did it matter? You got out of there before things turned into a full-blown argument."

Riwa sighed, knowing Urvi was right. "I wouldn't have fought with her. But... something about Tia just doesn't sit right with me."

Urvi finally met her gaze. "Then don't waste your energy on it. Some things don't need figuring out."

By the time they placed the last book, Riwa felt lighter. She admired how Urvi handled things—not with unnecessary words, but with action. Some arguments weren't worth fighting. Some people weren't worth the overthinking.

As they stepped out, the final bell rang, signalling the end of the day.

"Well, at least that was a good distraction," Riwa muttered.

Urvi smiled. "That's what friends are for."

And just like that, the day moved on, as it always did.

The morning air was crisp, filled with an unspoken energy as students settled into their seats. The usual hum of casual chatter was interrupted when the professor entered; his expression was unusually serious.

"I have an important announcement," he began. The class quietened. "Starting tomorrow, the military will be using our college premises for training and temporary refugee assistance. Since we are close to the Army base, it's a strategic location for them. This arrangement will last for about 20 days."

A ripple of whispers spread across the room. Some exchanged curious glances, while others sat up in anticipation.

"During this period, classes will shift online. After the training, the government has sanctioned funds for campus renovation, meaning you'll be attending online sessions for the next month."

At first, there was silence. Then—a wave of excitement. A whole month away from rigid schedules? Away from the suffocating routine of daily lectures? This was an unexpected gift.

"Since today is a half-day, you're free to leave after this period," the professor added, barely finishing his sentence before students broke into delighted murmurs.

"This calls for a plan," Astha declared, turning to the group. "We should go somewhere—what about the lake behind the college?"

"That lake?" Urvi raised an eyebrow. "I've heard it's stunning."

"Even better in the evening light," Anvi agreed. "Let's go."

Everyone nodded, their excitement growing. As they made their way toward the exit, Riwa felt a presence beside her.

"Riwa."

She turned to find a boy walking towards her, his posture relaxed yet assured. He had sharp, observant eyes and an air of familiarity that she couldn't immediately place.

"I'm Shitij," he introduced himself with an easy smile. "You're Riwa, right?"

She nodded, studying him. "Yes... Do we know each other?"

"We were in the same college during graduation, different sections, but I remember you from the debate competition."

Riwa tilted her head slightly, trying to recollect. Then she gave a small, polite smile.

"I figured we'd cross paths sooner or later," Shitij said. "We've ended up in the same course, same college—again."

She hummed in response, unsure of what else to say.

As they walked towards the lake with the others, Shitij continued, "So, do you enjoy teaching?"

Riwa paused, considering her answer. "It's fine," she admitted. "I like making things easier for students. And it's my passion."

Her words were honest, detached, but not indifferent. Shitij noticed that. She wasn't someone who spoke just for the sake of conversation.

Before he could say anything else, Riwa quickened her pace and joined Anvi and Urvi, subtly excusing herself from further interaction.

Shitij didn't mind. He only watched as she walked ahead, curiosity flickering in his gaze.

The lake was even more mesmerising than they had imagined. It stretched out before them, a serene body of water reflecting the sky, now painted in soft hues of orange and pink. The air smelled of earth and leaves, a fresh, natural scent that made the moment feel untouched by the outside world.

Some students scattered, taking pictures, capturing the beauty on their phones. Others sat on the stone steps leading down to the water, their conversations hushed as if afraid to disturb the peaceful rhythm of the lake.

Riwa, however, stood by the edge, her eyes fixed on the gentle ripples. She crouched down, picked up a single maple leaf, twirled it between her fingers, and then delicately placed it on the water's surface.

She watched intently as it floated, carried by the currents, drifting effortlessly, unbothered by direction or destination. Something about it fascinated her. How easy it seemed... to let go.

Shitij, who had been standing a short distance away, observed her silently. There was something different about her—something unspoken yet compelling.

She wasn't trying to be noticed. She wasn't the loudest in the group, nor did she demand attention. And yet, he found himself drawn to her in a way he couldn't quite explain.

It wasn't love at first sight. Not even an instant attraction. But there was something... something about her quiet intensity that made him want to understand her a little more.

As the evening deepened, the laughter of friends filled the air. But for some, like Shitij, a fleeting moment lingered just a little longer.

8
"Crossed Paths"

After weeks of silent screens and hollow online classes, the long-awaited message finally came: college would reopen on Monday. In her friends' group chat, Riwa spotted it first; emojis and excited messages exploded across the screen. After so many empty days, the thought of returning to the old corridors made her heart skip.

Monday morning broke clear and restless. Students flooded the campus, laughter ringing against faded walls. They swapped stories, their voices weaving together — half complaints, half nostalgia. Riwa smiled quietly, absorbing the familiar chaos she hadn't realised she missed so much.

The first bell shrieked through the chatter, calling them back to routine.

After a blur of lectures, the Head of Department entered, crisp and composed. A cultural talent showcase was announced; participation was mandatory, and a small fee was attached. Class representatives and coordinators were chosen swiftly, setting the machinery of excitement in motion.

Talk of sports and competitions swept through the groups like wildfire. Riwa's friends were already rallying for the Kho Kho tournament, their energy contagious. But Riwa stood back, smiling at their enthusiasm. Deep down, she knew that running and tackling weren't her game.

She turned over her options carefully, searching for her place – and found it, almost naturally, in chess. It wasn't loud. It wasn't fast. But it demanded the kind of quiet fire she knew she had.

Without wasting time, she walked over to the volunteers taking registrations. "Could you add my name for the chess competition?" she asked, a hint of quiet certainty in her voice. The volunteer nodded, scribbling it down and explained that there would be two phases — a selection round and a final. Riwa agreed, her mind already planning moves she hadn't played yet.

Across the room, she caught Saanvi's eye. Sharp, steady Saanvi, who needed no convincing. Grinning, she walked over and wrote her name down too.

Later that afternoon, the two girls borrowed a chess set from the sports room. They found a quiet corner where sunlight pooled across the floor and set up their board.

As pieces tapped softly against squares, Riwa watched Saanvi's quick, fluid moves with growing admiration. "You're good at this," she said, pushing a pawn forward.

Saanvi only smiled, resetting the pieces for another round. No need for words; the game itself spoke enough.

Riwa found herself struggling, the weight of the competition pressing heavily on her chest. Her mind raced with doubts—what if she wasn't good enough? What if she failed? But before she could spiral further, Saanvi caught her eye and gave her a soft, reassuring smile.

"Don't worry," Saanvi said, her voice steady and calm. "You might stand a good chance."

Riwa felt a flicker of hope, but her insecurities quickly crept back. She watched Saanvi, who seemed unfazed by her worries, and almost wished she could be as confident. But then Saanvi's words took a turn.

"I'll be absent during the competition," she continued. "I've got a diploma course and important classes to attend. But you've got this, Riwa. Go and make our department proud."

Riwa stared at her in surprise. There was no hint of jealousy in Saanvi's voice— only pure encouragement. It hit her like a soft, gentle wave. Women, she realised, didn't have to be competitors. They could be allies, lifting each other in ways that were strong, quiet, and profound.

Her doubt started to melt away, replaced by a feeling of gratitude. Saanvi wasn't just telling her to succeed — she was reminding her that this wasn't a race against each other. It was a chance to stand together, to support each other no matter what. Riwa felt a sense of camaraderie she hadn't fully understood before.

In that moment, her admiration for Saanvi deepened. It wasn't just the game or the competition that mattered; it was the bond they shared—one that wasn't defined by comparison or rivalry, but by mutual respect and a powerful sense of solidarity.

Riwa smiled, the weight on her chest lifting. She realised that Saanvi had just given her the most valuable lesson of all: true support comes not from winning, but from standing strong beside each other, no matter the outcome.

As the campus buzzed with excitement over the upcoming sports events, Riwa sat alone in the corner, the chess set in front of her. She had brought it from the sports room for practice, but a small sense of unease crept in as she set up the pieces. She was determined, but the quiet of the empty room felt strangely isolating.

Saanvi approached, her expression apologetic. "I'll have to leave early today. I've got some work at home and can only stay for half the day. You should practice with someone else."

Riwa nodded, her shoulders sagging slightly. Saanvi's absence left a noticeable gap, but she couldn't let it stop her. She began asking around, moving from group to group, but each person was absorbed in their preparations for the Kho Kho and basketball matches. Her frustration mounted as she realised no one had time to practice chess.

Just as she was about to pack up in defeat, a familiar voice interrupted her thoughts. "Having trouble finding a partner?"

Riwa turned to find Manas, the district-level chess champion, standing by with a knowing smile.

"Would you like to have a match with me?" he asked, his tone light but confident.

Riwa blinked, surprised. "Oh, Manas, yes, of course! But... do you know how to play?"

Manas grinned, his confidence unshaken. "Don't worry. I know how to play. If you lose, at least you'll know you lost to a chess champion."

Riwa couldn't help but laugh. Her earlier frustration faded, replaced by a surge of excitement. It wasn't just a practice session anymore; it was a chance to test herself against a real champion.

As Manas walked away, he threw a casual remark over his shoulder. "Practice harder, or you won't survive the first round."

The words hit Riwa like a slap. Pride flared in her chest, but deep down, she knew he was right. That night, lying awake in the dark, she replayed every wrong move, every careless mistake. The thought of failing gnawed at her.

The next morning, swallowing her hesitation, she found Manas by the sports hall. Her voice was steady, though her palms were cold. "Will you help me practice?"

Manas raised an eyebrow, amused. "I will, but only if you promise not to snap at me. You lose your temper faster than you lose a pawn."

A faint laugh escaped Riwa despite herself. "Deal," she said. "I'll keep my cool."

In that brief exchange, something shifted — not just a partnership, but the start of Riwa's real fight to win.

Riwa and Manas practised every afternoon, the chessboard between them a silent battlefield. Manas taught her more than moves; he taught her how to think.

"Chess isn't about the board or the pieces," he said once, moving a knight swiftly. "It's about two minds trying to outwit each other. Protect your king. Stay unpredictable. That's your real strategy."

Riwa carried his words like armour as the tournament day arrived. At the venue, she noticed only four girls had turned up. Curious, she asked a volunteer, who shrugged and explained that most students preferred faster games like basketball; chess had always drawn fewer participants.

As Riwa sat for her first match, she squeezed a pawn gently between her fingers, grounding herself. Victory came easily – her opponent was inexperienced – and Riwa advanced to the finals.

In the final round, the girl across from her smiled tiredly and said, "Let's finish this quickly. I barely made it through the first round. Looking at you, it's clear you'll win."

Riwa felt a flutter of nerves for a moment, but she quickly steadied herself.

I didn't come this far to doubt myself now, she thought, setting her first piece firmly on the board.

This match wasn't just about winning; it was about proving to herself that she belonged here.

Riwa was puzzled by her opponent's casual attitude, but she remained focused and claimed an easy victory, securing a gold medal and making her department proud. At the end of the day, as they walked toward the bus stop, Manas noticed Riwa's downcast expression despite her win.

"Why aren't you celebrating?" he asked, his voice laced with curiosity.

Riwa hesitated, then quietly confessed, "I wanted to win... but under real competition. I needed a challenge to prove all the effort I put in."

Manas smiled, trying to lift her spirits. "Why aren't you happy? It's not your fault the competition wasn't more difficult. Learn to appreciate what you've achieved."

Expecting Riwa to argue, Manas was surprised when she nodded and replied, "Maybe you're right."

Seeing the change in her demeanour, Manas teased, "Don't worry. We'll have a match together, and I'll lose on purpose just to make you happy."

A genuine smile spread across Riwa's face, softening her usual seriousness. Watching her, Manas felt something stir inside him, though he kept it to himself. He didn't want to rush anything; he valued building a strong friendship first. The budding feelings remained his secret, shared only with his mother when he got home.

That same day, Riwa shared the story of the competition with her mother. "I should treat Manas," she said thoughtfully. "He helped me a lot." Her mother smiled and nodded. "Of course, you should. He sounds like a good friend."

The next day at college, Riwa casually mentioned to Manas that she and some friends were heading to a café after classes. "You should join us," she suggested, unsure of how he'd respond.

Manas smiled, his expression warm. "I'll join you," he said easily. "I'll be there shortly after."

Just as Riwa was about to leave for the day, she heard a voice calling.

"Hey, Ved! How are you? Where have you been? Do you remember me? We met on the day of enrolment, and I haven't seen you since."

The voice took Riwa by surprise. For a moment, she stood frozen, a flood of emotions crashing through her. She didn't know how to react; her mind struggled to catch up with the unexpected encounter. Her body felt stiff, as if she were caught in time.

9

"A Friend's Promise"

The moment Riwa spotted Ved across the bustling college courtyard, her heart gave a startled leap.

He was here – not just in the same college, but, to her amazement, enrolled in the very same department.

How had she missed this before? How had he slipped past her notice all these days?

Lost in thought, she barely noticed the crowd shifting around her. As she made her way to her seat, she caught Ved looking at her. His gaze lingered for a moment longer than necessary, and she could almost see him preparing to walk over.

But before he could move, the shrill ring of the bell sliced through the air, calling everyone into the lecture hall.

Chairs scraped the floor, conversations ended mid-sentence, and the room quickly settled into the dull hum of a first lecture.

Riwa sank into her seat, but her mind refused to obey. The professor's voice became a distant murmur, lost somewhere in the thick fog of her thoughts.

She was utterly preoccupied – rehearsing, discarding, and rehearsing again a hundred ways she might start a conversation with Ved.

What if she made things awkward? What if he didn't even remember her properly?

No, she decided firmly, she wouldn't complicate it. This time, she would keep it simple – just a friendly hello.

An opportunity like this might not come again, and she wouldn't let her nerves steal it from her.

Excitement buzzed through her veins, so loud and wild that the lecture might as well have been delivered in a foreign language.

For the life of her, she couldn't catch a single word.

Riwa sat through the lecture, barely able to contain her excitement. She kept stealing glances at the clock, counting down the minutes until the short break — the perfect chance to finally talk to Ved.

The moment the lecture ended and the bell rang for the break, Riwa gathered her things quickly and made her way over to Ved's row.

Without hesitating, she slipped into the seat beside him.

Ved looked up, surprised, but his face immediately lit up with a smile.

"Hey! How are you?" he said. "I didn't even realise you were in the same college! I should've messaged you sooner."

Riwa's heart skipped. His words felt like music to her ears.

Wow, she thought, smiling back, barely managing to keep her excitement from showing too much.

Before she could reply properly, the bell rang again, signalling the start of the next class.

Riwa gave a small laugh and said, "Alright, we'll continue this during the lunch break. I should get back to my seat now."

"Sure," Ved nodded, grinning. "We'll catch up at lunch."

Riwa hurried back to her place, but concentrating on the second lecture was hopeless. Her mind wandered into soft daydreams—imagining Ved asking her for coffee, borrowing her notes, or just sitting with her under the big tree in the campus courtyard, talking for hours. She smiled to herself, already planning to offer him the neatly prepared notes she had worked so hard on.

Then suddenly, she remembered:

Oh right! We're supposed to get our semester assignment groups today!

A fresh wave of hope surged through her.

Please, let me be in Wade's group, she wished silently, twirling her pen between her fingers as the lecture faded further into the background.

The second lecture came to an end, and as the lunch break began, Riwa felt her heart beat a little faster.

She shifted her seat once again, carefully positioning herself close enough to Ved for a conversation, yet leaving just enough distance to appear casual.

As they both settled in, Riwa turned to him, her voice light but threaded with genuine curiosity.

"Where have you been all this time?" she asked with a soft laugh. "I don't think I've seen you in any of the classes before. It almost feels like today's your first day."

Ved smiled, the corners of his eyes crinkling slightly – a detail Riwa couldn't help but notice.

"No, it's not my first day," he said, his tone easy and warm. "I attended about 23 classes near the end of September."

Riwa blinked in surprise, piecing it together.

"Ah... that makes sense. I did take some leave around that time," she admitted, tucking a stray strand of hair behind her ear. "I guess we just missed each other."

"Exactly," Ved agreed, nodding.

The ease between them made Riwa's nerves settle slightly. She leaned in a little, eager to keep the conversation going.

"So, what have you been up to?" she asked, genuinely interested.

Ved's smile softened, becoming a little more reflective.

"I'm still figuring it out, honestly," he said. "Teaching interests me to some extent, but my main focus is on clearing the bank exams. That's really what I'm working toward."

He paused, glancing down at his hands for a moment as if weighing his thoughts before speaking again.

"I'm pursuing this teaching course mainly as a backup. The UP bank exam is coming up soon, and I needed to be here today to catch up, especially since the semester assignments are being distributed."

Riwa listened carefully, feeling a strange kind of admiration growing inside her.

Here was someone who wasn't simply drifting through life, but someone who had a clear direction – a plan.

It was rare, she thought, to meet someone so young yet so determined.

Without realising it, she found herself smiling – not just because of what he said, but because of the quiet conviction behind his words.

Meanwhile, Manas observed the conversation unfolding between Ved and Riwa, his gaze sharp and unreadable.

He couldn't help but notice the ease with which Riwa spoke to Ved – the natural trust in her voice, the effortless way she smiled.

A tight knot twisted in Manas's chest.

She never smiled like that with me, he thought bitterly.

Manas drummed his fingers restlessly against the edge of his notebook, pretending to be absorbed in his notes while catching every word between them.

He adjusted his seat unnecessarily, jaw tightening slightly as Riwa laughed softly at something Wade said.

He tried to reason with himself.

Maybe this was just their first meeting – pure coincidence.

Or maybe, he speculated uneasily, they knew each other from before, from a previous college, and were catching up on old memories.

A part of him — the part he tried to silence — whispered that maybe he was already too late.

The bell rang, pulling him out of his spiral.

The lunch break ended, and everyone settled back into their seats for the next lecture.

Later, as the teacher began announcing the semester assignments, Ved raised his hand, his voice steady but firm.

"Sir, may I ask something?" he said.

The teacher nodded.

"Why are we receiving our assignments so late?" Ved continued.

"In other colleges, assignments are given two months in advance, which gives students enough time to research and prepare properly. Here, we're being asked to complete major assignments within just one month. Wouldn't it be better if our college followed a similar approach?"

A murmur of agreement rippled through the classroom.

Manas glanced sideways at Ved, grudgingly admiring his confidence, but deep down, the knot in his chest only tightened further.

The teacher replied calmly, "I can't speak for other colleges. I know my students here, and I trust they can complete their work within the time I've given. I also provide all the necessary support to help them manage their assignments effectively."

Riwa shifted uncomfortably in her seat. While she understood Ved's point, she couldn't help but feel that he had spoken too bluntly. Still, she kept silent, recognising that it wasn't her place to interfere in a discussion between a teacher and a student. She focused on listening, understanding that sometimes it was wiser to stay out of matters that were not directly hers.

The conversation grew tense.

"If you have concerns," the teacher concluded sharply, "you're free to approach the management. I will grade the assignments according to my guidelines."

Ved leaned back, unbothered. "Alright, ma'am. I'll take it up with the management. No need to instruct me."

Riwa blinked, taken aback. Is this the same Ved I had a crush on? She wondered, her excitement dampening. His tone had been almost dismissive, and seeing him argue so coldly with a teacher unsettled her.

The room fell into an awkward silence as the lecture finally ended. Students packed up quickly, eager to leave.

Manas, who had been observing everything from the back, didn't say a word. He simply gathered his books a little too slowly, his fingers brushing over the edges of the table longer than necessary. As Riwa passed by, he acted as if he didn't notice her, eyes glued to the scribbles on his notebook. Yet, the slight clench of his jaw told a different story.

Outside the classroom, as groups of students dispersed, Manas approached Riwa briefly.

"I have some work nearby at my uncle's firm," he said casually. "I'll join you guys another time."

Riwa nodded politely. "Okay."

He waited a moment, half-hoping she would ask him to come along — but she didn't. She simply walked away without a second glance. Watching her leave, Manas felt a sting of confusion. She didn't even ask me twice. Sometimes I just don't understand her.

Riwa was searching for Ved. Her eyes scanned the corridor, but he was nowhere to be seen.

Across the courtyard, Manas stood leaning against the library wall, half-hidden in shadow.

He watched her search briefly, then turned away before she could notice him, disappearing silently down the opposite hall.

Classes ended, and Riwa assumed Ved had already left. She pushed the thought aside. He would be back soon; no need to worry. Despite her uncertainty, she felt a strange sense of joy, as though today had been one of the best days of her life. She smiled to herself, walking through the halls with a fluttering heart. It wasn't about reason or logic; love, she realised, was something felt deeply and passionately, not calculated.

Days passed, and Ved still didn't return. Riwa found herself checking each day, hoping he would show up. She assumed he was busy preparing for his bank exam.

One afternoon, the teacher asked Riwa to distribute the assignment documents to the class. As she forwarded them, a thought struck her. How can I make sure Wade gets this? She scanned the class register, finding his contact number. Without hesitation, she dialled his number, hoping he wouldn't be upset.

The phone rang, and after a few moments, VED's voice came through, cautious. "Hello?"

"Hi, Ved, it's Riwa from class," she said, steadying her nerves. "I just wanted to update you on the assignment. I know you're probably busy with your exam prep, so I thought I'd call to make sure you got the details."

There was a brief pause before he spoke again. "Thanks for calling."

Riwa smiled softly, relieved.

Ved's voice echoed through the phone. "Thanks for the update," he said. "I'm not home right now, but when I get back, I'll save your number and message you on WhatsApp."

Later that evening, a message appeared on her screen from Ved's WhatsApp: Hello, please forward the assignment details. Also, save this number—this is my WhatsApp.

Riwa smiled, quickly saving his number and sending the document over. His reply came swiftly: Thanks.

Her heart fluttered at the simplicity of his response, but she couldn't help herself. "How's the exam prep going?" she asked, eager to keep the conversation going.

"It's alright," Ved replied.

"When do you think you'll be back in college?" Riwa asked, wanting more from the exchange.

"Soon. Just need to handle a few things first," he responded.

Riwa nodded to herself, feeling a mix of disappointment and understanding. "Okay, take care," she decided not to push it further, letting the conversation end there.

Most of the students, overloaded with assignments, agreed to take a brief break, giving themselves the week to catch up on their work before diving back into the grind.

Riwa hadn't been to college for the past week, focusing instead on her assignments. Meanwhile, Ved had been attending classes, and after a few days, he messaged her playfully.

"Have you and your friends taken a TC from the college? Why haven't you been showing up?"

Riwa laughed at the message and replied, "No, TC! We just decided to take the week off to catch up on assignments."

Ved, curious about what Riwa had missed, responded quickly, "I see. Well, only about 10 students have been showing up. The teachers checked assignments and held half-day sessions. It was mostly revision, but honestly, a lot of the lectures turned into storytelling sessions about their past."

Riwa chuckled at the idea of her teachers reminiscing. "Sounds like an interesting week," she teased.

Wanting to keep the conversation going, she asked, "So, have you managed to finish all your assignments?"

Ved hesitated before replying, "Not yet. Still working on them. Hey, could you do me a favour and share your assignments with me? I'm missing some steps, and it would help if you could send them."

Riwa smiled, feeling a warm flutter at the request. "Of course! I'll send them over," she replied, her fingers already moving to gather the documents.

The next day, Riwa sent Ved a picture of the assignment, feeling a sense of completion. After a moment, she typed out another message.

"Are you coming to college today?"

Ved's response was quick. "No, I'm not coming today. I've been going for the past few days, so I'm taking a break. I'm exhausted." He added a laughing emoji, trying to lighten the tone.

Riwa sighed, her fingers hovering over the screen. She couldn't help but wonder why he wasn't coming. "He can't come today, and I'm going... How will things work like this?" she thought to herself.

Days passed, and Ved didn't show up for a single class. One evening, when Riwa returned home, her phone buzzed with a message from him.

"How was your day at college? Anything new?" Ved asked casually.

Riwa felt frustration rise in her chest. He had been absent for days but still wanted updates about assignments and college life. She paused, wondering if she should simply ignore the message.

But then, she replied, "If you want updates about college, you should come every day. I'm not here to give you daily reports. It's your responsibility to stay updated."

After sending the message, she hesitated, feeling guilty for being too blunt. However, she quickly typed another message, trying to soften her tone.

"I understand you're preparing for the bank exam, but are you going to handle college like this all the time? Today I'm helping you, but in the future, others might not be as willing to give you updates. You should think about that."

Riwa put her phone down, hoping she hadn't been too harsh. But a part of her felt relieved, finally standing up for herself.

Ved stared at Riwa's message, surprised by her directness. He hadn't expected her to react so firmly. It was clear now that he needed to be honest with her—she was someone who, despite her quick temper, cared deeply about understanding others. Taking a deep breath, he began typing his response.

"I haven't been completely truthful with you, Riwa," he started. "I mentioned preparing for the bank exam, but the truth is, I'm dealing with a serious health issue. I have blood clots in my brain, and I'm undergoing treatment. I can't attend college regularly because I need to visit the hospital frequently. Today, they admitted me after a routine check-up showed that my condition had worsened."

Ved paused, feeling the weight of his words. "I haven't shared this with anyone because I didn't want sympathy. I'm on medical leave, and the college management is aware of my situation. However, they still expect me to complete and submit my assignments on time. I've been telling people I'm preparing for the exams at home to avoid questions."

Ved sighed, the truth now out in the open. "I hope you understand my situation now, and please, I request that you keep this between us."

He hit send; his heart was pounding. The truth had been hard to share, but it felt like a weight had been lifted.

Riwa stared at Ved's message for what felt like an eternity. She felt a mix of surprise and guilt—guilt for her earlier frustration and for not understanding what he was going through. Her fingers hovered over the keyboard as she processed his words, unsure of how to respond.

Finally, she typed: "I'm sorry, Ved. I had no idea. Please don't worry. I believe you'll get through this. You're stronger than you think."

His response came quickly, almost too quickly: "Don't apologise. You couldn't have known. I hope so, too. Thanks for being understanding."

Riwa let out a breath she didn't realise she was holding. This wasn't the response she expected from someone who had been so distant. She paused for a moment, thinking about the right words. She finally wrote, "Focus on your health, okay? I'll make sure you get all the updates from college. Don't stress about assignments or anything else. You've got enough to handle." She added a smiley face, trying to lighten the mood.

"Thanks. I'll talk to you later," Ved replied. "I've got a check-up now. Take care of yourself, Riwa."

Riwa sat back, feeling a weight in her chest. The realisation of what Ved was going through hit her hard. She wasn't just talking to someone a bit absent from college— she was talking to someone who was fighting for his health. In that moment, she knew she couldn't just leave things where they were.

As she prayed that evening, her thoughts weren't on herself, but on Ved. God, please keep him strong. Please heal him quickly. A resolve formed in her heart. Ved didn't need pity; he needed support, a friend who would stand by him no matter what.

In her prayer, Riwa made a promise to herself. She would stand by Ved, not as someone special, but as someone who would never let him face these battles alone. She would be there for him through the silence, the pain, and whatever came next. And she was determined to keep that promise.

10

"Tying Hope"

Now that Riwa knows about Ved's condition, she regularly updates him on college life and checks in on how he's doing. Understanding that Ved doesn't like discussing his health issues, she avoids asking direct questions about it. Instead, she focuses on making their conversations feel normal. "Hey Ved, how was your day?" Riwa would ask, keeping the tone light and casual, never letting on that she was concerned about his health. "Did I tell you? It was Ma'am's birthday today, but she didn't give us a treat," she added teasingly. Ved responded with a laugh, " Don't worry about it. You can have your own treat with your friends!"

Riwa didn't talk to Ved every day, but she made sure to check on him regularly. Sometimes, Ved would respond quickly, while other times, it would take a week before she received a message from him. When a week passed without a reply, Riwa would feel a wave of sadness wash over her. She understood, though, that Ved might be busy or that his treatment and medication could be affecting his ability to stay in touch. She also knew that mood swings might be making things harder for him. But through it all, Riwa reminded herself that she needed to be strong, as Ved needed a friend who could truly support him.

A month had passed, and whenever any document needed to be submitted, Riwa would submit Ved's documents along with her own, using his roll number. It wasn't possible for Ved to return to college frequently, as he had been referred to AIIMS hospital in Rishikesh. While Ved remained there for treatment, Riwa took care of submitting all the necessary documents and assignments that the college required on his behalf.

One day, Riwa's parents planned a trip to Ayodhya to visit the Ram Mandir. Although the temple was still under construction, they were excited to see it. Riwa was in mixed emotions, but she kept her own feelings hidden. For months, her thoughts had been occupied with Ved, but she knew she couldn't burden her family with her emotions. She masked her pain and focused on being enthusiastic about the journey to Ayodhya.

The family had train reservations and travelled to Ayodhya for their much-anticipated visit. As they explored the nearby temples of Ram Mandir, Riwa's mother leaned closer and said softly, "You know, Shiv Ji's favourite is Nandi. If you whisper a wish into Nandi's ear, he might make it come true." Her words were filled with a gentle, hopeful tone, and Riwa felt a flicker of hope amid her hidden worries. Though she tried to stay cheerful, her mother's comment stirred a mixture of longing and hope within her, making the visit to Ayodhya even more poignant.

After hearing her mother's advice, Riwa approached Nandi with a mix of hope and earnestness. She whispered into his ear, "Please, take care of my family. My brother is in class 10; I hope he does well in his exams. Watch over my parents and keep them happy. Most importantly, please look after Ved. He hasn't replied to my messages for the past week, and I worry about him. I hope he is alright. Please help him recover soon and be well."

The Ram Mandir was a vision of beauty and elegance, offering a sense of peace and tranquillity as if soothing the very soul. It seemed that anyone seeking solace found it within the temple's serene atmosphere. Riwa also experienced a deep sense of inner calm there. After their visit to the Ram Mandir, Riwa and her parents went to the Saryu Ghat, where they continued to enjoy their time together.

Near the Saryu Ghat, many vendors were selling lamps. People would light these lamps and float them in the river, believing that their wishes would be fulfilled. Riwa and her brother also bought a lamp and lit it by the Saryu Ghat. While they both made wishes for their family's well-being, Riwa's thoughts were also with her dear friend Ved, who had been unwell. As she released the lamp into the river, she silently hoped that Ved would find not only happiness but also a renewed sense of health and vitality.

Riwa's faith in her devotion was unwavering. She was certain that Ved would return and recover fully. Despite the anticipated challenges, she held onto the belief that everything would turn out well in the end. As the family journeyed back home, they did so with cherished memories of Ayodhya. The warmth and hospitality of the people there were unforgettable. The profound devotion they exhibited for Lord Ram was awe-inspiring, and such a captivating experience could only be found in Ayodhya.

Love is a mysterious force that often sneaks up on us without our realising it. It doesn't need words to exist; its presence can be felt through actions and thoughts. While speaking about our feelings is sometimes necessary, love is not confined to verbal expression or physical presence. It manifests in the care we show and the prayers we offer for someone important. Love empowers and frees us, providing strength that transcends the limits of language. True love remains in our hearts, regardless of the distance. Even when apart, we continue to think of and cherish the one we love, with our hearts forever beating for them.

Riwa had fallen deeply in love, and her visit to Ayodhya only strengthened her belief in the power of true love. Witnessing the extraordinary bond between Lord Ram and Goddess Sita, she realised that genuine love remains unshaken by distance. Regardless of how close or far apart two people may be, true love endures. This profound lesson from their divine love gave Riwa renewed confidence in her own feelings, reinforcing her trust in the strength of her love.

The trip to Ayodhya came to a close, and everyone resumed their routines the following day. As Riwa settled back into her work, she received a message from Ved: "Sorry for the delay, Riwa. I got caught up with some work and couldn't reply earlier. I hope you're doing well." Riwa felt a wave of relief as she read his message. She quickly responded, "No worries at all. How are you? I hope everything is going well on your end."

Riwa settled into her chair with a sigh of relief as she read Ved's message.

Ved - "I'm doing just fine, actually."

Riwa: "That's good to hear! So, when do you think you'll be coming back?"

Ved: "I'll return as soon as the doctor gives me the green light. Right now, I'm just caught up here with some delays, but I'm confident everything will work out soon."

Riwa looked out of the window, the setting sun casting a warm glow over her room. She typed her reply with a reassuring smile.

Riwa: "I'm sure everything will be alright. Just keep your faith in God."

Ved

In the unfolding tale of Riwa and Ved, both are navigating their lives with their own aspirations and dreams. Ved finds himself sitting in the hospital garden, lost in thoughts about when he might return home and achieve the dreams he holds for himself and his parents. Meanwhile, Riwa waits for Ved, each of them clinging to strands of hope. Hope, after all, is what provides ordinary people with the strength to confront life's challenges each day.

One afternoon, as rain began to fall, Riwa, who was at home, gazed out the window of her room. The sight of the rain sparked a smile as memories of her first encounter with Ved came flooding back. She couldn't help but wonder if there might ever be a chance for Ved to fall in love with her. Riwa understood that Ved only saw her as a good friend, with no deeper feelings towards her. As the rain stopped and a vibrant rainbow appeared in the sky, Riwa reflected on the notion that some things are best left to destiny. Just as the rainbow displays its own array of colours, love also has its own unique shades. The fact that destiny had brought them together must mean something. After all, true love is the one that includes the anticipation and patience of waiting.

11

"Sibling Bond"

Riwa was studying at midnight when she suddenly noticed the calendar and realised that the New Year was only four days away. She then got up from her desk and went to the kitchen to make a cup of coffee. As the familiar aroma filled the air, she remembered that her brother was also studying, so she decided to make a cup of coffee for him too. She walked into the drawing room, where her brother sat, absorbed in his studies. The soft glow of the lamp highlighted the concentration on his face. She approached quietly and placed the steaming cup of coffee beside him. As he looked up, surprised but grateful, Riwa settled into the chair next to him. "So, what's up?" she asked with a warm smile. "How's everything going?" Her brother looked up, a hint of weariness in his eyes as he cradled the warm cup in his hands. "Just busy with studies and project work," he replied, his voice carrying a mix of fatigue and focus. "My board exams are starting in February, and to be honest, I'm pretty nervous about it." He paused for a moment, then glanced at her with a curious expression. "Did you feel the same way when your exams were coming up?" he asked, seeking reassurance in the shared experience of those intense, pressure-filled days. Riwa smiled and replied in a reassuring tone, "Every student has to face this pressure; it's nothing new. So don't be afraid of it. Remember, if you're honest with your efforts, the result doesn't define you. Your only duty is to give your best and not worry about the outcome. And don't worry—whatever the result, your sister is here for you. We'll figure things out together, so stay optimistic. And remember, never make a decision that you might regret later." Her words, calm and steady, were meant to comfort him, reminding him that he wasn't alone in this journey.

Then her brother asked, "So, Di, what's going on in your life? Have you found someone special in college?" Riwa replied with a hint of humour, "So you can tell Papa, huh?" "No, Di, I'm just asking," he said. "Well, I know about Ved. But honestly, I like Manas bro more than Ved. I think Manas bro is a better friend to you than Ved is." Riwa smiled. "Both are good. Manas is a great friend, and Ved is someone I care deeply about. But I think you should focus on your studies rather than on me. I can handle my own issues, you know." Her brother nodded. "Yes, Di. But don't stress too much. Ved will come back soon." Riwa gave him a final piece of advice. "Study well and get plenty of sleep," she said, and then left the room to return to her study table. As she sat down, her thoughts drifted to Ved. She considered sending him a message but decided it was too late in the night. She resolved to drop him a message the following morning.

The next morning, Riwa got ready for college and met her friends at the bus stop. After they boarded the bus and found their seats, Riwa took out her phone and sent a quick message to Ved: How are you? She knew Ved's habit of delayed replies, so she slipped her phone back into her bag and joined the conversation her friends were having. They were discussing skincare routines and various jewellery trends—topics that Riwa found herself genuinely interested in, which helped her relax and enjoy the ride. As they reached the college and waited for their class to start, Riwa's phone buzzed with a message from Ved. I'm fine, it read.

Ved then asked, "Are you at college?" Riwa replied, "Yes." Curiosity gnawing at her, she quickly followed up, "So, what did the doctors suggest?" A moment later, Ved's response came, heavy with the weight of his situation: "My condition isn't good. The doctors suggested surgery if necessary—to save my life." Riwa's heart sank, and tears welled up in her eyes. Unable to contain her emotions, she quickly got up and rushed to the library, seeking the quiet solitude she needed to process the news. After a few moments, once she had composed herself, Riwa replied to Ved, "Don't worry, everything will be fine. The New Year is coming, and with it, new beginnings will take place."

Ved simply smiled at her message. After spending the entire day at college, Riwa returned home, her heart heavy with worry. She quietly retreated to her room, her mood visibly low. Her mother, noticing her unusual behaviour, gently approached her. "Riwa, are you okay?" she asked with concern. At that, Riwa couldn't hold back any longer. Tears streamed down her face as she collapsed into her mother's arms, sobbing uncontrollably. "One of my friends isn't doing well," she managed to say through her tears. "He's in the hospital." Her mother held her tightly, offering a comforting embrace. With a reassuring smile, she said, "Don't worry, dear. Your friend will be fine soon. Just wash your face, be strong, and remind your friend to stay strong too." There was something special about a mother's hug—how it could melt away stress without you even realising it. Riwa felt a sense of calm slowly return as she rested in her mother's comforting arms.

Days passed, and soon they reached the last day of the year. It was nearly midnight, with just five minutes left until the New Year began. Riwa could hear the lively party music coming from a nearby restaurant, where the excitement was palpable. As the final moments of the year ticked away, the sound of people joining in a countdown filled the air, their voices growing louder with each number. The anticipation was electric, and when the clock struck midnight, cheers erupted as everyone celebrated the arrival of the New Year. Amidst the flurry of greetings, Riwa's phone buzzed with a message from Ved. "Happy New Year, dear. May you achieve all your dreams this year," he wrote, his words carrying warmth and hope for the days ahead.

Riwa blushed as she read Ved's message, a warm smile spreading across her face. She quickly typed back, "Happy New Year to you, too."

12
"May Time Stand Still"

On New Year's morning, Riwa found herself alone at home. Her parents had gone to the temple, and her brother was off to a friend's house to exchange New Year wishes. With the house quiet, Riwa decided to mark important dates on the calendar. As she noted the days, it suddenly struck her that in just three months, their teaching course would be complete, and they would all become facilitators. This realisation stirred up a mix of emotions within her. She couldn't help but wonder what the future held for her and Ved. Would they still stay in touch after the course ended, or would life take them on separate paths,

Riwa knew Ved's new medical report would arrive in two days and decided to wait before messaging him, her heart full of hope. As the anticipated day arrived, she could hardly contain her eagerness and sent Ved a message asking about his health. Moments later, Ved replied with a photo of his report and a joyful message: "The new reports are great! No surgery needed, and I'm recovering well. I'll be discharged in a month and can return to college." Relief and happiness washed over Riwa as she read the news, grateful that Ved was on the path to recovery.

Riwa is counting the days until Ved arrives at college. The long-awaited day finally arrived, but that morning, Riwa overslept and missed her bus. By the time she realises, her friends have already reached college. In a panic, she tries calling Anvi to see if she has left, but Anvi doesn't answer. With Ved having left for college early, Riwa is left wondering how she will get there alone. Despite never having travelled alone by bus before, she gathered courage and boarded one. As she is on her way to college, she informs Ved of her situation. Ved, concerned, asks her if she is alone. Riwa confirms she is, and Ved advises her to be careful.

Riwa replies, "Yes." Finally, she reaches college and runs to her class. As she enters, the first lecture is in progress. With a slight, apologetic tone, she asks, "May I come in, Sir?" The professor notices her and questions, "Why are you late? Don't you know the college timings?" Riwa replies, "I'm sorry, Sir." The professor tells her to settle down quickly and not to disturb the class. Riwa finds a seat and begins to look around for Ved. Spotting him in the last row, she smiles and then turns her attention to the lecture.

Soon after the lecture, Riwa approaches Ved and asks how he's doing. Ved replies that he's fine and happy to be back at college. He thanks Riwa for taking care of everything in his absence. Riwa smiles warmly and asks about his plans now. Ved shares that he had recently taken a tech exam and applied for an internship with a company, aiming to become a renowned app developer. He explains that he enrolled in this course mainly because of his mother's concern during his illness. Initially, he hadn't given it much thought. However, throughout his treatment, he discovered his true passion for computers.

Riwa smiled and said, "That's great news! When will the results be out?" Ved replied, "Probably next month." Then Ved turned to her, asking, "How are you doing?" Riwa's eyes lit up. "I'm doing great, actually. I can't even put into words how happy I am to see you back here." Ved looked a bit confused by her response but chose not to dwell on it. As class ended, everyone headed to the bus stop. Anvi and Tiya stopped at an ice cream parlour for a treat. Samarth and Manas decided to join them. Riwa and Ved were left alone. Ved asked, "Do you want to join them?" Riwa shook her head. "No, I'm okay. What about you?" Ved sighed. "I'll pass too."

As Riwa and Ved boarded the bus, Riwa felt a surge of happiness sitting next to him. Ved began to share stories with her, his excitement palpable. "After my recovery, I went rafting," he said, pulling out his phone to show her videos and photos from his trip. "I also visited some beautiful temples." Riwa watched the clips with fascination. "It looks amazing! I'm glad you're doing so well." Ved smiled, then added, "Oh, and you won't believe this—one of the girls from our class messaged me. She told me she likes me and even sent a video of herself singing a song to confess her feelings." Riwa's eyes widened in surprise. "Really? That's quite a bold move." Ved nodded, chuckling. "Yeah, it was unexpected. I wasn't sure how to respond."

As the bus ride continued, Riwa and Ved became so engrossed in each other's company that they barely noticed when they reached their destination. Ved turned to Riwa and asked, "So, will you be coming to college tomorrow?" Riwa smiled and replied, "Yes, I'll be there. What about you?" Ved said, "I'll message you about my plans later." Riwa nodded. "Okay, sounds good." With a warm smile, she added, "Bye for now."

Ved smiled back and replied, "Bye."

After returning home, Riwa eagerly awaited Ved's message, but hours passed without any word from him. Growing tired of waiting, she decided to message Ved to check if he would be coming to college the next day. Ved replied, "No, I won't be coming tomorrow."

Riwa read the message and typed, "No problem."

Riwa felt a pang of disappointment upon reading Ved's message. She had been looking forward to spending each day with him, and the thought of missing even one made her feel unsettled. Despite her feelings, she knew she couldn't do anything.

A week later, the college internal exams began, and attendance

was compulsory for all students. Riwa sent Ved a message, saying, "The internal exams start next week, and we need to attend them." Ved replied, "Please let me know the exam schedule as soon as you have it."

As they both immersed themselves in preparation, finding time to meet became challenging. One day, while heading home on the bus, Riwa and her friends noticed all the seats were occupied. The only seat available was exposed to the harsh sunlight.

Ved was also with them and suggested, "Riwa, just sit at the back. The back seats are unoccupied, and the sunlight isn't reaching there." Riwa looked around and asked, "But there are six of us and only four seats available. Where will you sit?" Ved replied, "Don't worry about me. I'll sit here. You and your friends go ahead and join your group. I'll be fine." Riwa hesitated, "Are you sure? The sunlight is really intense." Ved reassured her, "Yes, it's okay. Just go and be with your group. I'll manage."

Riwa told her friends, "Let's sit at the back." She began to step back slowly to make sure all the available seats were filled. Ved noticed her and asked, "Why aren't you heading to those seats? If all the seats are taken, you'll end up with nowhere to sit." Riwa smiled and replied, "I'll manage. Besides, with the crowd, I'm not getting a chance to move anyway. Don't worry about it."

All the seats were filled, leaving only two bathed in direct sunlight. Ved took one of these sunlit seats and sat down. He turned to Riwa and said, "Are you sure you want to sit here? You should have moved to the back earlier to get a better seat. Now you're stuck with this sun-bathed spot." Riwa smiled warmly and replied, "Since this is the only one left, I'll sit here."

Soon, they met Ved's brother's friend on the bus, and the conversation shifted to lively discussions. As Ved chatted with his friend, Riwa found herself lost in her thoughts, smiling as she watched him intently. When Ved noticed Riwa and asked the reason behind her smile, Riwa quickly changed the topic, saying, "Look at how beautiful those flowers look from this window."

Ved looked around and asked, "Where are the flowers you're talking about? I don't see any." Riwa replied, "Maybe the flowers have just passed by. You might have missed them." Ved found her answer a bit odd but shrugged it off, thinking to himself that the sunlight might be getting to her.

Ved simply said, "Okay, next time you see them, let me know, and I'll check them out too." He turned back to his conversation with his friend, while Riwa quickly added, "Sure, I'll let you know." Riwa then focused on Ved, enjoying the moment and feeling happy as she observed him, content with their time together.

13

"Heart Vs mind"

Riwa entered the classroom where Sanvi and Ved were talking to each other. She then went to her seat and began revising for the exam.

Saanvi: "Hey, what's up? All done?"

Riwa: "Yeah, I hope so."

Saanvi: "Even I'm not sure about today's exam."

Riwa: "Hmm, today's exam is quite tough."

Saanvi glanced at Riwa and said, "Yeah, and I didn't get a chance to study yesterday. Next week, my sister's baby shower is going to be at our house, so we've been busy picking out gifts for her in-laws."

Riwa nodded sympathetically. "I see. So, what's your conversation with Ved about something important related to the exams?"

Saanvi shook her head. "Actually, Ved and I were discussing the new developments in AI technology."

Riwa's eyebrows lifted in surprise. "Oh, I thought you two were talking about today's exam. Well, tech topics are a bit beyond my brain's syllabus."

Saanvi offered a reassuring smile. "Don't worry, you're doing great in all your fields." Riwa just smiled in response, feeling a bit more at ease. Later, as they waited for the bus after the exam, Ved turned to Riwa with a bright smile. "You know, my tech exam results are out, and I've been selected for the internship! As soon as this course is over, which should be within a week, I'll be joining the company." Riwa's eyes widened in surprise. "You're going so soon?" Ved shook his head with a smile. "Not really. I'm quite late for this opportunity because of my health condition."

Riwa asked, "So, where is your company?"

Ved replied, "In Bangalore." Riwa's face lit up.

"That's superb!"

Ved then noticed something. "I see you also have something to share with me."

Riwa nodded. "Yes. We finally found a house that meets all our requirements, and we'll be buying it soon. The deal is done, so we'll be moving into our own home—no more living in a rented place."

Ved smiled, "That's great."

Riwa smiled at Ved. Ved said, "So, tomorrow, Sir is going to announce the internal exam marks."

Riwa nodded. "Yes."

The next day, Sir announced the marks:

Anvi: 12/20

Samarth: 15/20

Saanvi: 14/20

Riwa and Manas: 17/20.

Ved 15/20

Riwa and Manas were quite pleased with their scores; both had achieved the highest marks in class.

However, Ved was visibly upset with his internal exam marks. After class, he went to the staff room to discuss his concerns with Sir. Meanwhile, Riwa's friends were planning to go to a coffee shop and invited her to join them. Riwa, who was waiting for Ved on the college campus, told her friends to go ahead and that she and Ved would join them there. In the staff room, Ved was engaged in a heated discussion with Sir about his marks. Despite Ved's arguments, Sir seemed determined not to lose the argument. After a tense exchange, the HOD decided to grant Ved an additional point. Meanwhile, Riwa had been sitting alone and waiting for Ved on campus for about half an hour. When she finally saw Ved approaching, she moved to talk to him. However, Ved suddenly veered left, avoiding her. Riwa's heart ached at the sight, but she understood that Ved needed to be alone at that moment. Although she wanted to comfort him, she decided it was best not to interfere and quietly left him to his solitude. Later, Riwa arrived at the bus stand instead of the coffee shop, where her friends had also gathered to catch the bus. Anvi asked Riwa, "Where is Ved?" Riwa replied, "He had some important work to finish, so he stayed back at college." Anvi then suggested to Riwa, "You should propose to Ved as soon as possible." Riwa's face brightened with a smile upon hearing this. Later, when Riwa was cooking dinner at home, she reflected on Ved's behaviour today at college. Despite her thoughts, she decided to set aside her concerns and planned to propose to Ved on her birthday. Since her birthday was the day after tomorrow, Riwa decided to think about how to propose to Ved. At the same time, she wondered whether Ved would remember her birthday.

As midnight approached, Riwa eagerly awaited the start of her birthday. When the clock struck 12, her phone buzzed with a message from Ved: "Happy Birthday, dear. May all your dreams come true." — Ved. Riwa's heart warmed at the thoughtful message, adding a special touch to the beginning of her day.

No doubt, Ved had remembered Riwa's birthday and was the first to wish her. The next day, Anvi and Samarth planned a surprise birthday party for Riwa.

After class, they invited Riwa to the café, but they forgot to inform Ved about the party. After finishing her work in the library, Riwa headed to the café. As she arrived, and everyone burst into song, singing "Happy Birthday" for her. Riwa's eyes scanned the room, searching for Ved. Noticing her look of confusion, Anvi explained, "Sorry, yaar, we forgot to inform Ved about today's party." Riwa's disappointment was evident as she asked, "No problem. Do you know where he is now?" Anvi apologised again, "Sorry

about the mix-up." Riwa, seeing Anvi's sincere efforts, reassured her, "No problem. Let's just cut the cake and enjoy the celebration." As the party continued, Anvi questioned

Riwa, "Do you think Ved is so busy that he didn't plan any surprise for you? He didn't even make an effort to make your day special. Don't you think that's a bit selfish of him?" This time, Riwa was left speechless and didn't know how to respond. She simply replied to Anvi, "Yes, he is busy. He's about to move to Bangalore, so he's just arranging things." Anvi nodded, "Well, it's

your and his matter. I won't interfere. Later, Manas approached Riwa and wished her a happy birthday. "Thanks," Riwa replied warmly. Manas then asked, "Don't you think loving Ved is quite difficult? Don't you think you've taken a long and perhaps the wrong route?"

Riwa smiled and replied, "In love, there's no such thing as a long or wrong route. If two people truly want to be together, they'll find a way. Don't worry, I'm fine." At the same time, Riwa was contemplating Manas's words, though she kept her thoughts hidden. She knew that if she wanted to pursue a relationship with Ved, she would need to be patient. However, she couldn't help but feel disappointed that Ved wasn't there for her on her birthday. Despite this, she resolved to remain hopeful and look for another opportunity to propose to him. After the party, Riwa received all the pictures and posted a few from the celebration. Ved then sent her a message, saying, "I saw you celebrating with your friends. I wasn't involved. Am I not your friend?" Riwa explained the whole situation to Ved, noting that he seemed quite disappointed. She added, "I wasn't sure what went wrong, but I'm sorry if I hurt you." Ved responded, "No problem, dear. There's no need to apologise. It wasn't your fault. I hope next time we can celebrate your birthday together. Relax, and happy birthday once again." Riwa replied with a smiley. In her heart, she pondered if Ved was really upset with her on this small topic. 'What was my fault if he left early without meeting me? He could come to me and ask if there was any plan, or he could have contacted Anvi. He knows that Anvi is my friend. As a friend, Anvi planned a surprise for me. Why can't he plan? Is he really selfish? Did I love the wrong person? Was Manas right? Should I take time before making any decision related to Ved?'

Riwa questioned herself and thought that he made me apologise on my birthday, even though I was not at fault. Is this relationship possible? Will my love reciprocate in the right way? She messaged Anvi for her advice. Should she propose to Ved? Anvi replied, "See, we don't know the outcome until we act." After reading this, Riwa thought about confessing her love to Ved, not thinking much about the response.

14
"Chasing The Future"

It was the last day of practicals, marking the final day of college. Riwa was in good spirits, having gotten ready on time that morning. Just as she was about to leave, a message from Urvi popped up on her phone: "Hey Riwa, today's the first day of my period, and I'm dealing with some pretty bad cramps. Could you wait for me? I don't want to take the bus alone. Please, will you wait for me?" Riwa read the message and quickly replied: "Of course, I'll wait for you. Don't worry—just let me know when you're feeling up to it, and we'll go together."

After a moment, Urvi replied, "I'll be about 10 minutes late." Riwa responded quickly, "No problem at all. Just get ready—I'll wait for you. But if possible, try to hurry up a bit."

Shortly after, Riwa received another message from Ved: "Hey, where are you? We're all here—Anvi, Samarth, Manas, and Riya have already arrived at the bus stand. I'm with them, and we've been waiting for the bus for about 5 minutes. We're all set to go together. Where are you? Come quickly."

Riwa found herself in a dilemma. She wanted to be with Ved, but she didn't want to leave Urvi to face the bus ride alone. She was deeply torn, contemplating whether to stay with Urvi or join Ved since it was the last day of college, a chance she didn't want to miss.

When Riwa reached the bus station, she saw the bus pulling away. She tried to signal it, but it was too far. Despite her frantic sprint, she hoped that Ved might have gotten off the bus to wait for her. Urvi, running behind Riwa, was also trying to catch up as Riwa pursued the departing bus. Together, they finally reached the bus stop, breathless and hopeful.

With hope in her heart, Riwa called Ved and asked where he was. She wanted to know if he was still at the bus stand. Ved informed her that he was already on the bus. Riwa, surprised, asked, "Didn't you get off to wait for me?" Ved replied, "No, actually, everyone was already on the bus, so I boarded it as well."

With a heavy heart, Riwa replied, "Okay." She thought that Ved had taken the bus because Sanvi was on it and hadn't stayed behind for her. Riwa questioned herself, wondering if that was the true reason, and if Ved liked Sanvi. Urvi then informed Riwa that the next bus would arrive in 5 minutes, and they could take that one. Riwa simply nodded, lost in her thoughts.

After a while, the next bus arrived. Riwa and Urvi boarded it. Riwa was not in the best of moods, but she was determined to make the most of the day. Urvi, noticing Riwa's demeanour, asked if she planned to propose to Ved.

Riwa, convincing herself, replied confidently, "Yes, I will propose to him today." As Riwa's mood brightened, Urvi, intrigued, asked how she planned to propose. With a spark of excitement, Riwa reached into her bag and pulled out a small box, showing it to Urvi.

Riwa opened the box and showed the gift to Urvi. Urvi's eyes widened as she saw the present and exclaimed, "This gift is awesome!" Riwa smiled and blushed; her excitement was evident.

After showing the gift, Urvi asked Riwa about her decision regarding the job offer from the HOD. As one of the top facilitators, Riwa had received a campus placement opportunity to teach at the school affiliated with the college. "Will you take this opportunity?" Urvi asked. Riwa took a deep breath and replied, "My decision depends on Ved's response to my proposal. If he says yes, I'll consider relocating to Bangalore. I'll find a job there, and together, we can make this relationship work."

As she spoke, a flicker of uncertainty appeared in her eyes, reflecting the weight of the decision she faced.

Soon, Urvi and Riwa arrived at the college. The atmosphere was bustling with activity as everyone focused on binding their documents and organising their project work meticulously into file folders.

Riwa approached Anvi and they exchanged greetings. Afterwards, Riwa began binding up the projects, her gaze wandering occasionally as she looked around for Ved.

Suddenly, Ved entered the classroom and called out, "Hey Sanvi, what did you write in the internship file's conclusion?" Riwa's anger flared at Ved's behaviour. She wondered why Ved was asking Sanvi about the conclusion. After all, he had received the entire assignment from her, and he was asking what to write in it from Sanvi. Yet today, his focus seemed solely on Sanvi. Riwa couldn't understand why.

Sanvi looked at Ved and suggested, "Why don't you ask Riwa? She's the one who shared the assignment with both of us. She'll explain it better than I can." Ved paused and then nodded in agreement. "You're right. Riwa, could you tell me what you wrote in the conclusion?"

Riwa then patiently explained the entire assignment's conclusion to Ved. After that, the roll call began, with each student called up according to their roll number for the viva and the final assignment submission.

As the viva concluded and the day progressed, it naturally turned into a scribble day, with everyone writing notes on each other's T-shirts and shirts, filling the air with laughter and memories.

Ved stood quietly in the corner, a faint smile on his face as he watched the scene unfold. Sanvi noticed him standing there and, after a moment, approached him. "Ved," she began casually, "aren't you going to write a note for Riwa? She's been a good friend to you in college." Ved glanced at her, his expression giving nothing away. "No," he replied, almost as an afterthought. "I can't put in the effort after today. I'll leave her without a note." Sanvi stared at him for a moment, unsure of what to think. Ved didn't elaborate, and the conversation drifted into silence after a brief pause.

Riya, who had been nearby, turned to Ved. "Ved," she asked, "should I write a note for you?" Ved shrugged, his tone casual. "No, don't bother. I don't know anyone that well, so I'll just skip it."

Riwa, who had been quietly listening, was deep in thought about how to propose to Ved. She decided she would do it on the bus ride home. As the party wrapped up, everyone gathered for a final group selfie, exchanging best wishes and promising to stay in touch. The mood was a mix of nostalgia and hope. Afterwards, Manas approached Riwa and asked about her plans. "Riwa," he said, "what do you have in mind for the future?" Riwa shrugged and smiled. "The future is uncertain. What we plan doesn't always happen, so I just want to enjoy the present." Manas nodded, agreeing. "Yes, and I want

to enjoy this moment with you," he said warmly. He then asked, "Won't you write a note for me?" "Of course," Riwa replied. "You've been a friend who's stood by me." They shared a heartfelt moment of friendship, savouring their connection before parting ways.

As the group boarded the bus heading to their hometowns, Riwa had hoped to sit with Ved. However, Ved chose to sit with Sanvi instead, leaving Riwa surprised and a bit hurt. She took a seat with Riya, trying to mask her disappointment. The bus ride was filled with animated conversations about future plans and reflections on the party. Anvi and Samarth nestled together, making promises to stay in touch—vowing to talk twice a day, meet monthly, and make more sweet commitments. Across the aisle, Riwa's gaze kept drifting to Ved and Sanvi, who were engrossed in conversation. The murmur of

their exchange was inaudible from her seat, but Ved's focused attention on Sanvi left Riwa feeling unsettled. Her carefully laid plans seemed to unravel, and a deep sense of disappointment weighed heavily on her heart.

As the bus approached Ved's stop, Riwa realised she had only moments left to speak with him. Despite feeling overlooked throughout the day, she decided to make her move. Riwa made her way to Ved. "Ved," she said, her smile a mix of sadness and resolve, "today is our last day to see each other for a while. I wanted to say goodbye properly." Ved looked at her and replied, "Yes, I am excited to go to Bangalore and achieve my dreams. I wish you all the best, too." Riwa reached into her bag and pulled out a small box, handing it to him. "This is for you," she said. "When you get home and have a moment, open it." Ved stared at the box, puzzled. "What's this?" Just a small gift," Riwa said

softly. Before she could say more, the bus reached Ved's stop. He gathered his things and, with a brief nod and a simple "goodbye," stepped off the bus. Riwa watched him leave, feeling a profound sense of finality as the moment vanished.

That night, after dinner, Ved opened the gift box to find a classic pen engraved with his name and a note that read:

Dear Ved,

I wish you all the best and hope you have a great professional career and friends in your new journey. I believe you have the qualities of a great leader and will excel. Stay safe, take care of yourself, and always be happy and healthy. May God be with you.

From Riwa

Ved felt a mix of emotions and messaged Riwa: "Thanks for the gift. I'll keep the pen with me always, and the note is really meaningful. Thanks again."

When Riwa read his message, she was overwhelmed with tears. The contrast between Ved's words and actions struck her deeply. She spent the night crying, feeling that her love had been in vain and coming to terms with the painful realisation that her feelings were not reciprocated.

Two days passed without any contact between Riwa and Ved, and she knew he was scheduled to move to Bangalore soon. Suddenly, a loud crash from the kitchen made her rush over. She found her brother had accidentally broken her favourite cup. Overwhelmed with anger, Riwa yelled at him. Later, as Riwa retreated to her room, her mother noticed her unusual anger. Softly opening the door, she asked, "What's going on? What's bothering you?"

Her mother embraced Riwa tightly, her voice gentle yet firm. "Sometimes, things fall apart to make way for something better. Just as the broken cup makes room for a new one, your heartache is making space for real love and someone who will truly value you." She continued, her eyes filled with understanding, "Ved cared for you as a friend, and that's something to hold dear. Even though things didn't turn out as you had hoped, your ability to love so deeply is a testament to your strength. Keep that love in your heart and be proud of your courage and the purity of your feelings. It shows that you have the strength to give love selflessly, without expecting anything in return."

After soothing Riwa, her mother gently wiped the tears from her cheeks. "My dear, it's time for you to take the first step toward your future. Taking the first step means setting aside the immediate pain and focusing on what lies ahead."

Think about your career, your dreams, and the future you envision for yourself. This is your opportunity to embrace what will bring you fulfilment and joy. I'm not insisting you accept the HOD's offer, but if it's something you're genuinely interested in, you owe it to yourself to explore it. Don't let the past or the confines of this room hold you back."

Riwa listened intently, her mother's words resonating deeply. "Thank you, Mama, for always supporting me," she said, her voice gaining strength despite the lingering emotion. "I'll certainly consider the HOD's offer and think about what's best for my future."

Her mother nodded in understanding and said, "Riwa, lunch is ready, and we're all waiting for you. Come down quickly."

Riwa smiled, feeling a bit more uplifted. "Yes, Mama, I'm starving like a rat! I'm coming right down." Her mother left the room, heading to the kitchen to prepare lunch, while

Riwa took a moment to gather her thoughts before joining her family.

Riwa then picked up the phone and called the HOD. "Sir, I wanted to let you know that I'm accepting the job offer," she said. The HOD responded, "That's great, Riwa. Come to the school tomorrow to complete all the formalities." Riwa replied, "Thank you, Sir. I'll be there on time."

The next day, Riwa arrived at the school to finalise the job offer. She completed all the formalities and was officially allowed to join the school the following month. The sense of independence and the opportunity to pursue her dreams filled her with satisfaction. As Riwa stepped out of the school, her phone buzzed with a message from Ved. He had shared a thoughtful reel with her. When she opened it, the accompanying message read:

"Please, God, take care of her. I always want to see her happy."

The heartfelt words stirred a mix of emotions in Riwa.

Riwa replied with a simple "Thank you."

She then asked, "Have you reached Bangalore?"

Ved responded, "I'm taking the flight to Bangalore today."

Riwa replied, "It was nice meeting you. Have a great journey ahead."

Ved's response was warm and brief: "Thanks ☺."

After a long pause, Ved opened the group photo—the one where they were both standing together at the table.

He zoomed in slowly, his eyes tracing each detail, before zooming out again, as if savouring every moment. A soft smile tugged at the corners of his lips, but there were tears in his eyes, the kind that only memories could bring.

He whispered to himself, "Some things are better left unsaid."

With that, their conversation—and their shared chapter—came to a close.

www.ingramcontent.com/pod-product-compliance
Lightning Source LLC
Chambersburg PA
CBHW031309130726
47988CB00007B/2784